THE SMURFS TALES

Peyo

PAPERCUTZ™
NEW YORK

THE SMURFS TALES #2

"Smurfette In Charge"
BY PEYO
WITH THE COLLABORATION OF
ALAIN JOST AND THIERRY CULLIFORD FOR THE SCRIPT,
PASCAL GARRAY FOR THE ART,
AND NINE CULLIFORD FOR THE COLORS

"The Smurfs and the Book that Knows Everything"
BY PEYO
WITH THE COLLABORATION OF YVAN DELPORTE AND
THIERRY CULLIFORD FOR THE SCRIPT, ALAIN MAURY FOR THE ART,
AND NINE CULLIFORD AND STUDIO LEONARDO FOR THE COLORS

"The Bodoni Circus"
BY PEYO
BASED ON AN IDEA BY PEYO WITH THE COLLABORATION OF
PEYO AND GOS FOR THE SCRIPT AND WALTHÉRY FOR THE ART

Joe Johnson, *SMURFLATIONS*
Bryan Senka, *LETTERING SMURF*
Léa Zimmerman, *SMURFIC PRODUCTION*
Matt. Murray, *SMURF CONSULTANT*
Lily Lu, *SMURF INTERN*
Jeff Whitman, *MANAGING SMURF*
Jim Salicrup, *SMURF-IN-CHIEF*

HC ISBN: 978-1-5458-0719-4
PB ISBN: 978-1-5458-0720-0

PRINTED IN MALAYSIA
OCTOBER 2021

Papercutz books may be purchased for business or promotional use. For information on bulk purchases please contact Macmillan Corporate and Premium Sales Department at (800) 221-7945 x5442.

DISTRIBUTED BY MACMILLAN
FIRST PAPERCUTZ PRINTING

SMURFETTE IN CHARGE

There! My flowerbed looks absolutely smurfing with these pansies.

Now I just have to smurf them a little water...

What--? For smurf's sake!
Is something wrong, Smurfette?

I'm smurfing the handle, but the water's not smurfing out!
Hmm... I see what's smurfing!

You do? What's the problem?
Oh, a technical smurf. It'd be a little difficult to explain it to you...

But don't you worry. I'll come smurf it soon.

Difficult to explain to me! What, does he think I'm too smurf to understand?!

Meh, let's forget that. A walk will do me good...

Hello! What are you going to paint?
The dining hall. We have to smurf the work before this evening.
Z
1

I'm going to smurf you a hand!
Are you kidding me? You'll smurf paint on your beautiful dress.

No, I'll put on overalls.
Overalls?! Come on, that's no outfit for you.
That's right, Smurfette... you're way more smurfing like that.
?

What's wrong with all of them?! This is getting asmurfing!

And where are you smurfing? Into the forest?
We're going to smurf some wild strawberries deep in the big ravine.

I love wild strawberries! Wait for me, I'll smurf a basket and be right back.

But it's too dangerous. We might smurf face to face with a wild animal.
He's right! It's no place for a Smurfette.

Don't you worry, we'll smurf you some strawberries when we return. Make some super cold lemonade for us.
And maybe some cookies that you smurf so well.

Did you hear that, Papa Smurf? They take me for some feeble creature with nothing in her smurf! A doll who's good for nothing but wearing beautiful dresses and smurfing cookies!

Calm down, Smurfette! You know they're not being mean. But I recognize their minds are a little smurf sometimes...
!

You should smurf them another image of you. And I may have an idea how to do so...
?

This strawberry pie is delicious!
Yes, but the smell of paint is smurfing my appetite.
No, Dopey Smurf! I asked you for sugar... that's the smurf!

My young Smurfs, I have something important to smurf to you.
TING TING

I'm leaving tomorrow to visit the mage Homnibus. We're going to smurf some important research.
Oh, yeah?
Again?!

In the past, unhappy circumstances have often smurfed during my absence. Therefore, this time, I've decided to smurf someone in charge who will replace me.
Someone in charge?
Who?

I still haven't smurfed my choice. I'll smurf you my decision before I leave.

Someone in charge! That's new!
It'll be a difficult smurf to make.
Meh! Let's smurf our trust in Papa Smurf.
Any pie left?

It'll be me! I'm the smartest!
I'm the most inventive, smurfing up with solutions for all problems.
Me, I have a firm hand! I'll be respected.
Good ol' farming sense, that's what's needed for making good decisions.

I'm already running the kitchens... Why not the village?

Now, an hour of running! And get smurfing!
Yes, Hefty Smurf.

I'm smurfing a lecture tonight! No absences allowed! Understood?
Yes, Brainy Smurf.

3
You two, dish duty!
Right away, Chef Smurf.

All right! I'm ready, and the stork is waiting for me.

And what have you smurfed about the... Um....
Oh, yes, my stand-in!

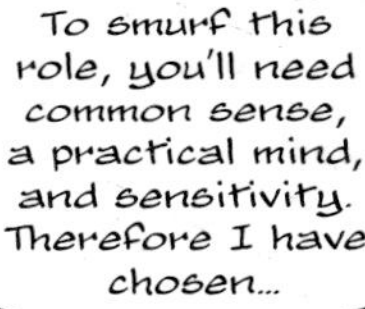
To smurf this role, you'll need common sense, a practical mind, and sensitivity. Therefore I have chosen...

...SMURFETTE!
Huh?!
For smurf's sake!
Is this a joke, Papa Smurf?

Not at all! I smurfed my decision a lot of thought and am counting on all of you to respect it!

Now, I must go! Smurfette will smurf you the schedule for the day.
Uh... Have a good trip, Papa Smurf!
And most of all come back soon!

Smurfette! What's smurfed into him?
He fell on his smurf!
Sure, she's charming and everyone adores her...
But Smurfette running the village is nonsense!

Hmm!

I don't mean to hurry you, but Papa Smurf said you must smurf some urgent work on the dam...

Yeah, yeah, we're on our way!
We know what has to be smurfed!
We're not kids anymore!
4

Wow… they seem smurfily put out!

⇒Hmpf⇐ it'll pass! They won't keep pouting for very long.

Let's see what yummy thing Chef Smurf is going to smurf up for us today…

Frankly, I don't understand Papa Smurf!

Usually I respect his decisions. But with this, I don't know what smurfed into his head.
CRAC
POC

Bah! In my opinion, he just smurfed that out of kindness to make Smurfette happy.
You think so?

Sure thing. But she shouldn't be giving us orders.
Oh, yeah, no way!
5

Z

HEY! GET UP!
Huh?
?

Get to work, or else Smurfette will come smurf you an earful!
HA!HA!HA!
That's mean.

I'm making a smurf stew, the chef's special.

I'm going to serve it with mashed chestnuts, smurf pears, and lentils.
Ah, yes... They'll have a hearty smurf.

You know, you could also smurf some lighter dishes sometimes. Grilled foods, salads...
Hmm! I'll think about it...

But until further notice, I'm still the one who smurfs the menus.

-Pff!- What attitude, that Chef Smurf!

They're so grumpy. This can't smurf on like this.

I have to smurf something to put them in a good mood. And I know what!
6

You understand, Smurfette, they think you're trying to run their smurfs... they can't wrap their smurfs around that.

No way!? It's still not smurfing!

Handy Smurf, you haven't smurfed my pump.
I was busy at the dam, Smurfette.

Wait, I'll smurf you a hand.

You see, Smurfette, there are some jobs best left to Smurfs!

I can smurf them to your home, if you like...
No worries! They're not even heavy!

BAM

SLAM

Well, now!
Ever since she was put in charge, she's been in a smurf of a bad mood!
8

>Sniff!< I'm wasting my time... They'll never smurf me seriously. And, what's more, they're getting mean.

Help!
His head is completely smurfed!
?

What has smurfed?! An accident?

It's Greedy Smurf. He smurfed his head through the window to see if there were any preserves left in the storeroom...
And now he can't smurf it out of there.
Gluttony is a wicked vice, and you always reap what you smurf!
?

NO! NOT WITH A HAMMER!

I'm not going to smurf you on the head, idiot! I'm going to smurf the wall all around the window.
And afterwards, I'll smurf the frame with my saw.
NO! NOT WITH A SAW!

Wait! There's another way to smurf him out of there! I was just smurfing my wash, in fact.
Your wash? What's the connection?

Look! First, I'll soap up his smurf...
Owwie!
That won't smurf anything, Smurfette, he's completely stuck.

9
You, lift him and turn him over. You have to smurf him on his back.
?

Oww! Ouch!
Quiet! We're turning!

And now, you're going to pull! One... two...
Help!

THREE!
SWOUP

I... I'm out! And nothing is smurfed!
Good job, Smurfette! He smurfed out in one shot and is in good shape.

You see, you just have to smurf his ears in the right direction, and he'll pass through.

Thank you so much, Smurfette! You smurfed my life!
Come on, you're exaggerating.

Not at all! Did you hear those two brutes? They were going to smurf my head off!

Smurf-ette's idea was awesome.
We turn him over and smurf! That's all there was to it.
Oh, that trick's as old as the smurfs! I'd just thought of it myself.

I think I smurfed some points with that.

Okay, let's not lose smurf. There's still hope!
10

The next day...

NOK
NOK

Hello, Brainy Smurf. I've brought you Baby. I'm going to go smurf a look at the dam.

Umm... today doesn't really smurf for me.
But it's your turn. You don't like baby-sitting him?

No, but I have the text for a lecture to smurf and--
YOU'RE SMURFING THAT JUST TO ANNOY ME!

WAAAAH!

It's all right, Baby. Smurfette is a little tense. Those responsibilities weigh very smurfily on her.
Sniff!

Grrr! That Brainy Smurf is starting to smurf on my nerves!

Smurfette, wait up!
11

I smurfed you some candy. It's to thank you for smurfing me out of that window.
Oh! Thanks, Greedy Smurf.

Uh... there aren't many left! I smurfed a few on my way here.
It's all right. Hee hee! It's the intention that smurfs.

Now, let's go see how the work is smurfing.

?
Hey! It's moving! Smurf the ladder tight!

It's easy to say smurf the ladder tight! It's slippery!
Anyhow, it's too short! You can smurf down from there!
ZWIIIIIP

Let me do it. I'll smurf there with the rope ladder.

Good one, Hefty Smurf! And the trowel? And the bucket? Are you going to smurf them in your pocket?!
Uhhhh...
12

Are they trying to repair the leaks?
Yes! The question is how to smurf to them?

Those leaks are a smurfy problem. Now, if I think about Baby Smurf's diapers...
? Baby's diapers?
NOC NOC

Could you smurf me a square of canvas this big? And a bit of rope?
!
?

Perfect! Now, call Hefty Smurf!
FLAP

Hefty Smurf, could you lie down here, please?
Lie down? I don't have time to smurf a nap!

Come on, be nice. For once, smurf what I tell you.

There! Hup! Now like this...
Hey! What?!

Wahaaa! The bouncing baby!
You dare make fun of me?! If you weren't a Smurfette, I'd--
Calm down, calm down! You'll see...
Pffff!
!

You see? That way, you'll be able to smurf the leaks safely...
No way! I look rismurfulous!

Come on, don't be childish... Unless you're afraid?
ME, AFRAID?!

Smurf me the bucket and trowel! We'll see if I'm afraid!
13

Hey, you know... this system smurfs like a dream!
Honestly, Smurfette, I don't know how you smurf up with such ideas.

"And I'll finish my speech, my dear Smurfs, by smurfing these few words to you..."
AROOO! AROOO! AROOO!

Not so loud, Baby. You're smurfing my concentration.

BOUM
BADAM
CRAAAC

I can't believe it! What are they smurfing?
BODOM
BODOM

Stop that racket right now, or I'll give you a good kick in the--
CRAC
CROC

...smurf!
SNORT!
14

AHHHHH! HELP!
What? Did you see a mouse?

!
NFF NFF

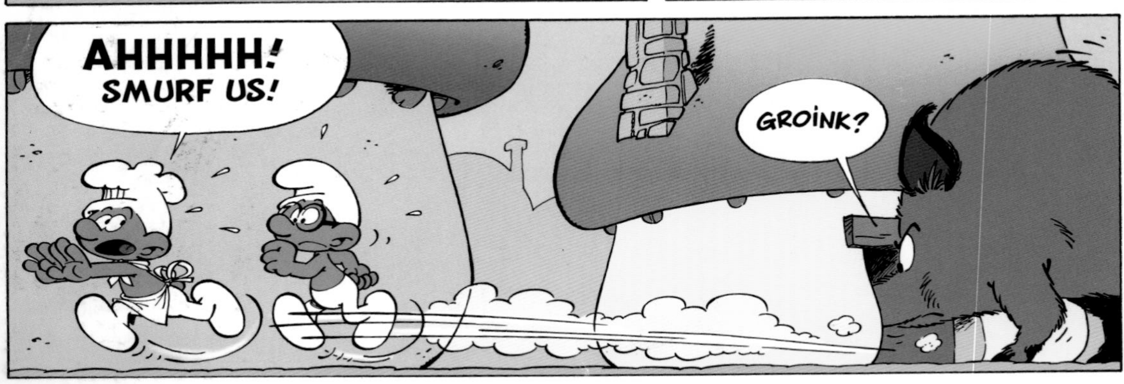
AHHHHH! SMURF US!
GROINK?

And the work is already smurfed! Thanks to you, Smurfette.
What if we still smurfed a little party?
Yes! That's a good idea after all.

Smurfette, it's terrible!
?

That dang-smurf-it boar came into the village!
And refuses to leave!

Baby Smurf! Did you smurf him somewhere safe? Where's Brainy Smurf?

15

Here we are, Smurfette! I waited for the boar to go away to smurf through the garden!
Whew! You're both safe and sound! What a relief!
Adada! Hee hee!

We have to chase that brute from the village. Everyone grab sticks and we'll smurf him a scare.

A stick? Do you think so?
A boar is smurfily big.
He could flatten us like pancakes.

Wait... That animal must have a reason to be smurfing like that all around the village.

Take Baby back. I'll go smurf a closer look...
No, Smurfette! He's going to smurf you to pieces!

I don't think so. And besides, it's not a "he," it's a "she."
Really?

GROINK?

What is she smurfing?
I don't know what she's got in mind!
Smurfette sure is a brave one.

KRRR
FROUTCH
Noise in the storage room? Someone forgot to smurf the door...

Just as I suspected!
CRUNCH
CROC
16

That's enough, you little porker!
Oink?
CROC
CRAC
CROC

Okay, get out of here! Your mama is smurfing everywhere for you!
Oink!

Groink?
Oink!

You see? She wasn't enraged, just crazy with worry.

OINK! OINK! OINK!
GROINK!

That's touching... -Oink!- I mean... -Sniff!-

OINK?
OINK!
GROINK!

Good job, Smurfette! You smurfed us out of real fix.
But how did you guess?
Oh! Female intuition.
17

Now that everything is back to smurf, I'm going to do my ironing.
We're going to get ready for the party.

You know what? We were smurfily unfair towards Smurfette.
That's true. She's a lot smurfer than she looks.
And you can smurf on her when there's a problem.

I say we smurf her a surprise for the party. Listen up...

Yes, that's a smurftastic idea!
We don't have much time!

Let's smurf fast over to Tailor Smurf's.

I think I've smurfed it this time. I've proven myself.

I'm looking forward to telling Papa Smurf about it. He'll be proud of me.

NOK
NOK

Smurfette, we've come to smurf you a present.
A present? That's so nice!

You're really too smurf! I can't wait to see what it is!
18

Oh, a dress! But it's...
Yes! Quick, go try it on!

Uh... I'm deeply smurfed... But I don't want to smurf Papa Smurf's place or even resemble him.

Late that night...
POUEEET
Me, I don't like "poueeets"!

Are you coming to dance, Smurfette?
Uh... I'm a little tired.

It was a really smurf day. I think I'm going to bed...
Oh. Already?

Goodnight, everybody! Have fun!
Goodnight, Smurfette!
Sweet smurfs!

Nobody can see me... Now's my chance!

I should've waited till morning, but I'm too impatient.

Luckily, it's a clear night. You can smurf as plain as day.

Ah, I'm here!
That's his fire!

Papa Smurf!
Smurfette? You, here, at this hour?!

I hope nothing serious has smurfed!
On the contrary. I have good news to smurf you.

I impressed the Smurfs so much, they wanted to name me "Mama Smurf," but don't worry, I said no... Hee hee hee!
Good job! I was sure you'd succeed.

It was hard, you know? At one point, I wanted to forget everything and come smurf you.
Fortunately, you stayed strong. You never smurf anything without perseverance.

You can come back now. They'll be all smurfed once they find out you were here all the time.
I'm going to stay here till dawn, Smurfette.

You see that bright dot? It's a comet tail smurfing overhead. And it's a perfect night for observing it.
A comet tail? That's funny! Name it "Smurfette"!

I'm going to call it "Mama Smurf" instead.
Oh, you're going to make me blush! It's time I get back...

See you tomorrow, Papa Smurf!
Goodnight, Smurfette! See you tomorrow!

The next day...
I'm going to smurf Papa Smurf a nice breakfast. He must be up by now.

Hee hee hee! I can't wait to see the Smurfs' faces when he explains the trick we played on them.

Hello, Smurfette! Hey, I smurfed a little inspection of the suspension bridge and I think we should--

Oh, you'll see about that with Papa... Well, we'll see about that later.

Papa Smurf has smurfed his shudders... Is he still asleep? Or maybe he wants to smurf them a surprise!

Papa Smurf? It's me!

He's not up! But he never smurfs late, even when he works the whole night.

Papa Smurf! Yoohoo!

Oh! He didn't come home.
22

I don't understand. What's he still smurfing on that hill?

Hey, about the bridge...
Not now, Handy Smurf, not now!

He did say: "until dawn." I have to go smurf on this.

PAPA SMURF?

Oh, my! He's gone.

But where could he have smurfed while carrying his stuff?

Near the spring, you can smurf tracks in the wet ground.

Here are the prints from my heels. And here are Papa Smurf's coming back down.

So, he went in the direction of the village. But he didn't come home!

!
23

Papa... Papa Smurf's bag! And the grass has been smurfed by big feet...

Oh! And here...

Big flat feet... Red hairs...
GARGAMEL AND AZRAEL!

Ahaaaa! So it's true that passing comets are signs of extraordinary events.

We captured a Smurf... And not just any old Smurf: Papa Smurf himself!

When I saw the little fire twinkling on the hill, I immediately thought: "There's a Smurf up there!"

But I wasn't going to approach over open ground! No, I hid near the spring. I waited patiently...

And hup! I snatched you up as you passed by! And people say I'm not clever?!

Ohhh... No way! Who would dare say that?

24
Right, make fun of me! You won't be laughing once you go
IN THE KETTLE!

It's awful. Gargamel has smurfnapped him! I have to smurf the alarm in the village!

But, if Papa Smurf is in danger, there's not a moment to lose... Ohhh, I don't know what to smurf!

Oh, well, I'll hurry to Gargamel's! I'll go smurf help later!

So, you want to cook me? That's a weird idea, I'm very tough.
Come now, don't play dumb.

You know that Smurf broth will allow me to make the philosopher's stone and change lead into gold.

Ha! Ha! That's ridiculous! Where did you come up with that?
I read it in one of my books of spells!

No serious grimoire would contain such nonsense.
Really? Wait, I'll show you.

Drat! Great timing coming to bother me now!
NOK
NOK
NOK

YES, what do you--
?!

Mail?
25

"The Order of Sorcerers"! What do they want now? I've already paid my dues!

"As a result of multiple complaints concerning you, we've decided to come inspect your facilities...

"...and to verify your basic knowledge!"
GOAT DROPPINGS! THAT'S TERRIBLE!

What nerve! I'm renowned for leagues in every direction!
That's the problem!

"The test will include a practical exercise and a closed spell book test on potions and spells"!

Closed spell book?! But I don't know all the formulas by heart!
No? You disappoint me.

What?! You think you're smarter than me, dwarf?!
Oh, I'm not saying that! But, still, I have a few centuries of experience...

That's the solution! The panel will come tomorrow... You're going to help me study!

I'm finally here! I hope nothing bad has smurfed!

Me, help a sorcerer? Never, Gargamel, never!
Papa Smurf's voice! Whew, he's alive!
26

Listen... if I pass my test, I'll forget about turning you into a broth.
Ha! Ha! And I should believe you?

I swear! On... on the head of my dear Azrael!
Your stupid cat? You're joking?!
?

Then, to the devil with the exam! I'll cook you by the first beams of the sun just like the spell book says!
Oh! That's horrible!

Please, Papa Smurf, say yes!

Oops!
?
!

SMURFETTE, LOOK OUT!

EEEEEE!

Why... what a nice surprise!
PLOP

AZRAEL! NO!

Not now, Azrael!
CLAP
27

Meanwhile, at the village...
Hey, have you seen Smurfette?
Uh... no, why?

I've been needing to talk to her since this morning about a problem with the suspension bridge...
Well, maybe she went to smurf a look at it.

PFFF!... Mama Smurf or not, she doesn't have any sense of organization!

And now there's two, Papa Smurf! The situation has changed!

In the pantry, we have a succulent Smurfette! And in front of the door, a big, famished tomcat...

So, you'll help me study, or she'll be cat food for Azrael!

All right, I have no choice. But once you've taken your test, you'll let her go!
Cross my heart!

I have no trust in you. But I hope that, for once, you'll keep your word!
You insult me! A sorcerer has his honor!

Okay, now that everything is settled, let's get to work!

Oh, yes... We must clean up around here too.

This should do the trick!

There! Clean all this! Azrael will keep an eye on you!
PFF! They're all the same!

I'm sure your potion would have an effect... But it's no good for inspiring love!

*The Idiot's Guide to Stupidity

At the village...
I'm telling you, I looked everywhere for her. I don't know where she could have smurfed. And nobody has seen her.
That really is worrying.

Okay! I'll gather everyone, and we'll go smurf for her!

Tell me the recipe for the ointment that protects against fire.
Whoa! What a test.

I'd put in... uh... stinging nettle juice...
Hmm!

And dragon scales too, dried salamander powder and... and phoenix droppings!
No, no! You're making stuff up! I can tell we'll spend all night on this!

SMURFETTE?
YOOHOOOO! SMURFETTE!

She's not answering us. I don't know what else we can smurf.
The situation is very serious. We have to go get Papa Smurf.

You're right! At dawn, I'll smurf to Homnibus's home.

The protection invocation is Beelzebub, Moloch, Mammon, Zabayon... No, Zagueron, Zanyreason and Z...Z...ZZZZ...
Go to bed, Gargamel. We can't do anymore.
Z
Z

The next morning...
Hey, a stork! Do I have visitors?

Yes, it's my friends the Smurfs! How are you?

There's a serious smurf in the village! We came to get Papa Smurf!
Papa Smurf? But he isn't here.

What?
When did he leave?
Let's see... I haven't seen him in months.

Well... now I don't understand anything at all.

Gargamel, stop fretting so! Save your energy!

I'd like to see you in my place! If I'm kicked out of the order, I'll have to work for a common healer's fee!

You have to help me give the right answers!
How?

I'll put you behind them! Give me signals!
But that's cheating.

Who cares?! Forget your morals and think of Smurfette!
-Sniff!-

31
A horse... They're here!
CLIPPETYCLOP
CLIPPETYCLOP

A desolate location... a perfectly dismal cottage...
Yes, the ideal setting for a sorcerer!

Gargamel, I presume? We're the inspectors from the Order of Sorcerers.
Uh... Yes, come in.

Hello? What is that creature?
A blue elf! That wouldn't be a "Shmoot"?

I found it in the forest! Unfortunately, he's old, sick... and completely senile!

Let's get to the reason for our visit. As you know, the Order has received various complaints concerning you...
Honestly, I don't know what I'm being criticized for.

Let's see... We have the case of that peasant who wanted nice hair so he'd be attractive...
Well?! He got it!

That's true... But since then, he's been suffering from chronic hiccups!
Hic Hic Hic Hic Hic
A... a regrettable side effect!

And the young lady who wanted to see her Prince Charming appear?
Beauty is subjective, you know.

And that knight you were supposed to make invincible?
Mommy...
Uh... A slight error in dosage!

If you like, I have other cases I can remind you about...
No, no! That won't be necessary!

Since you have no further objections, we'll start the inspection.

Hmm! I must admit this is rather clean.
Yes... There are just enough spider webs to create atmosphere!

Our colleague also possesses a splendid assortment of toxic, foul, and poisonous ingredients.
A lot of them have expired, I think. But check...

Let's start the practical examination. You're going to make a potion in front of us and test it on yourself!
Gulp!

Gladly! But sit down here. You'll see better!
?

Please prepare for us... invisibility lotion!
No... no problem!

It's very simple. I get... Uh... What do I get again?

One moment, it'll come to me. I know it like the back of my hand.
Yes, yes...
So they say!

Ah, got it! Sesame oil, aloe, resin of... styrax...
?!

Serpentine, oxymel, sticklewort, and slug juice!
Uh... Exactly!
SESAME OIL
ALOE
STYRAX RESIN
SERPENTINE
OXYMEL
STICKLEWORT
SLUG JUICE
33

Everything is ground and mixed! Now, the spell... INVISIBLUSGOINGUNSEENUS!

Let's see if it works.
Uh... Yes, there...

!
The test is conclusive!

May... may I wash my hands?
Go ahead!

We just have a series of questions left to ask you...
What, more?

It won't take long! They're multiple-choice questions.
Oh! Perfect, I love those!

Let's see... Which stone is associated with the planet Saturn: opal, sapphire, or topaz?
Sapphire, of course!

Which plant is called "rooster spur": peony, sage, or verbena?
Child's play! It's peony!

What is the best painkiller: earthworms, rabbit droppings, or dried stink bugs?
Rabbit droppings!

Good job, esteemed colleague! A perfect grade! Without the slightest hesitation this time.
Oh, you know, once I get going...

You've passed our test!
But our Grand Master has the final decision! And the complaints against you are serious...
34

Just between us... If you give him that interesting creature, it could play strongly in your favor...
Papa-- the old Smurf?

That bothers me a little. I need him to... Well, I'm very attached to him.

Now that I think about... I'm stupid!
SMAK

I have another specimen in the armoire! I'll give you that one!
GARGAMEL! NO!
What... it speaks!

Let's say it jabbers a little still... But the other one is in perfect health!
Mpff!

Hup! This one's in the armoire, and I'll give you her!
Oh! It's a female?

GNAP!
YEOWWWW!

You see? She's full of energy! Ha! Ha! Ha!

Take this one. The Master will be very happy with her. What's more, she's charming.
You dirty smurf! We should smurf you in the smurf!
What is she saying?

There you go, safe travels! Thanks for your visit! And give my regards to our revered Master!

35
Gargamel, you're a despicable traitor!
Why's that? I promised to let her go... And I kept my word!

This little Shmoot will amuse the Master!
It's "Smurfette," you ignoramus!

The return trip will be long. We should've come by broomstick.
You know, my dear, with my arthritis...

I'm not sure... Which way did we come?

I don't remember! All these roads look alike!

Please don't smurf the left one!
Oh? Why not?

That road smurfs towards the house of a horrrrible witch!

Ha! Ha! Ha! She's so funny!
But, little thing, we're sorcerers too!

I know! But Pustula is really frightening! When I think of her, it smurfs me goosebumps!

Pustula, Pustula... that doesn't ring a bell! And I can't find her in the Order's directory!
But she's famous! People smurf from far and wide to buy her potions and poisons!

She's not a member of the Order and sells potions?!
Without paying her dues! Or her sorcery sales tax? We'll have a word with that Purula... uh, Petula!
36

Please, don't smurf to her home! When she gets mad, she's terrifying!
Oh, yes? I'm trembling already! Ha! Ha! Ha!

Well, what? Does the road stop here?
Yes, you have to continue on foot. And the terrain is dangerous. Smurf back!

Out of the question! You'll guide us!
She mustn't escape! I happen to have a bit of rope here...

Come on, show us the way.
You asked for it!

That Pustula lives far from everything. I'm surprised people come this far...

I don't see any path anymore.
It's this way!

AAAAAH!

By Beelzebub! A bog!
My files!
I told you: the terrain is dangerous! And with your weight...

Don't worry, it's not deep! You'll end up smurfing out of there!

By the way... I smurfed a mistake! There's no witch named Pustula!
Oh, the little fiend!
37

This is disgusting! What's the spell for rising into the air?
Like I know that by heart?

Hee! Hee! Hee! I got those Smurful sorcerors!
?

Poor Papa Smurf! He's still in Gargamel's clutches!

I'm close to the old mill. That's too bad! It'll take me hours to smurf to the village!

Now that I think about it... on the roof of the mill, often there are...

Yes! They're there!

At the village...
Smurfette has disappeared, Papa Smurf, too... I can't make head or smurf of it!
That's right. I don't know what we can smurf.
Uh... What if we put a new smurf in charge?
Oh, don't start driving us smurfy with that again.

YOOHOO, SMURFS!
?
38

Because of the comet with a tail, Papa Smurf refused to smurf back to the village with me, and Gargamel saw the fire and he smurfed him to make a broth out of him, but luckily, he had to take a test and he's so stupid, and I smurfed them in the bog, thanks to the witch Pustula who doesn't even exist, and here I am!

Oh! That's clearer! You see, when you smurf correct syntax, you--

Smurfs, I've chosen you to smurf a raid on Gargamel's home.

We'll enter through windows and chimney simultaneously. He won't know what smurfed him!

Handy Smurf, we'll need a powerful catapult to smurf the windowpanes.
Hmm... I'll go see what I can smurf...

You, Jokey Smurf, prepare an explosive that makes lots of smoke!
Count on me, it'll smurf! Ha! Ha!

You three, you'll smurf through the chimney by sliding down the length of a rope.
Easy!
Smurf's play!

But practice anyway! If the kettle is on the fire, you'll have to avoid smurfing up inside it!
Oh, yeah... that's true!

Hey, Hefty Smurf, are you sure that--
Don't you worry yourself, Smurfette. I've got the situation well in the smurf.

AAAAAH!

Yeesh... Why did you smurf on those masks?
Well... So Gargamel won't recognize us!

Go ahead! Let yourself smurf and stop just above the ground!

YEEHAW!

BOOOM

You smurfed! You're in the kettle!
Drat!
40

Look out, I'm going to test my smurf-gas bomb!
Pshheeeee

BOOOM

Pee-yew! That smurfs horrible, but it's not making any smoke!
Hmm... did I smurf the wrong formula?
Smurfs & Pranks

Look... I smurfed some wheels on this old seesaw.
A seesaw?

Smurf the target closely and admire the precision!

?

!

Handy Smurf, are you okay?
Yes! Just some fine-tuning to be smurfed...
Listen, this won't smurf like this! I have a simpler plan--

Sorry, Smurfette! This kind of mission is Smurfs' work! And we don't have the time to smurf about it!

Fine! If that's how it is...

SLAM

There you go! Now she's pouting again.
What an attitude. You can't smurf her anything.
41

Look at this dress... You're the ones who smurfed it to me! Am I the Mama Smurf, yes or no?
?
Uh...
Yes!

Then, listen to me! Here's my plan: we're going to Gargamel's. You'll stay hidden while I smurf alone towards the door...

When Gargamel opens it, I'll lure him outside. That's your chance to smurf into the house to free Papa Smurf.

But you, Smurfette? Gargamel might capture you!
Trust me, I know how to smurf myself out of there.

You want to save Papa Smurf? Then, let's forget the equipment, training, and debates, and let's smurf action!

Smurfette is right... united we smurf! Let's rally around her red cap!
Yes, let's go!
Hurray for Smurfette!
Papa Smurf, here we come!

You got to admit it, she's a real leader of Smurfs.
Meh, if I had long blond hair and a tiny dress, I'd lead them around by their smurfs too.
Oh, yeah? Try it!

Oh, wait a moment! I have to smurf home real quick!

I forgot my purse!

Are you smurfing me? Her purse! To go free Papa Smurf!
42

For your last meal, I went to find you some sarsaparilla. And people say I have no heart.
Poor Gargamel... People are so mean.
Z

He's right, this is no doubt my final meal. Who could smurf me out of here?

So, as soon as I draw Gargamel away, you smurf into the house!
Understood, Smurfette!
Good luck!

YOOHOOOO, GARGAMEL!
!?

HUH? SMURFETTE!?!

Smurfette is back? Then all hope is not smurfed!

What?! Those stupid sorcerers let you go?
No, I smurfed away from them! Your Grand Master won't get me, nyah!

Him, maybe not... but ME, I will!
EEEEEK!

Move out! It's up to us to smurf!

PAPA SMURF, WHERE ARE YOU?
Here, in the armoire!

43
AAAH! AZRAEL!

HELP!

Hang on! You have to smurf his attention!

Easy for you to say!

My little Smurfs! What a joy to see you again!
Let's smurf out of here fast, Papa Smurf! Gargamel isn't far away!

I... I can't keep going!

Oh, no! He's going to get smurfed alive!

SMURF THE DOOR, QUICK!

CLAP

Okay, he's locked up! You smurfed a good job!
MEOOOW!
HFF! *PFF!* Thanks... *HFF!* *PFF!*

We did a really good smurf!
But where's Smurfette?
Oh, smurf! That's right... Smurfette!
44

So, little poppy! Did you think you were faster than me?

He caught her! Let's all smurf on him together!
Not so fast. Let's see what smurfs.

So, you escape and come back here just to mock me? You'll pay VERY DEARLY for that!
I'm not afraid! You'll see how bravely a Smurfette dies!

But before that, let me powder my nose! I want to smurf looking beautiful!
?

Powder your nose? Ha! Ha Ha! That's a Smurfette idea!

Pffft!
!

AHHH! MY EYES!

PEPPER! IT'S PEPPER
You got it, Gargamel!

Smurfette, you were awesome!
HURRAY FOR MAMA SMURF!
Thanks, I'm very smurfed... But let's not dawdle here!

Those voices outside!? The Smurfs!

I'm going to flatten you, microbes!

BAM

I'll... get... revenge! Oww!
Meooow!
45

So, you smurfed pepper in your compact?
Oh, yes, Hefty Smurf! A Smurfette has more than one trick up her sleeve.
Let's smurf back via the suspension bridge, it's shorter.

NO! NOT VIA THE BRIDGE!

HUH?
AHHH!

Good job! I tried to smurf you that there's a problem with this bridge!

Smurfette, you smurfed yourself to be a hero-- Uh, A heroine! You deserve your new dress a thousand times over.
Thanks, Papa Smurf. I think it's a bit much for smurfing. I'd rather change clothes.

We're smurfing a big party this evening, Smurfette. We're counting on you.
Gladly! But I have to hurry. Ironing, dishes... I have lots of things to smurf.

Work or not, I'm very happy to smurf back to a normal life.

Oh! My pansies are all smurfed! I have to water them.

HANDY SMURF!
Yes, Smurfette?

46
Hey, the pump still isn't smurfing...
Oh, yes, that's right! I'll smurf it later. The bridge needs repairs.

There you have it! Everything really is back to smurf!
End

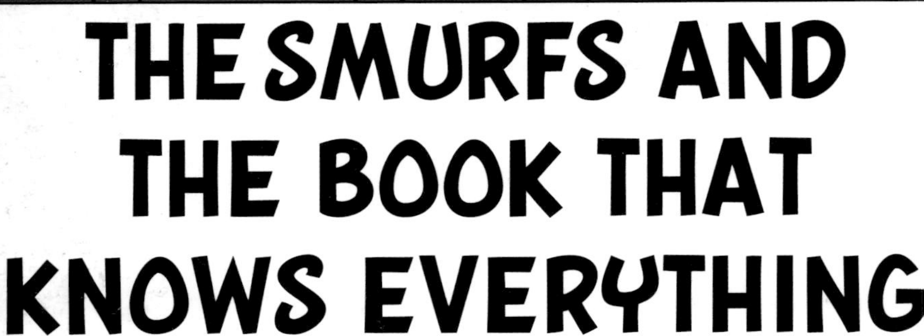

THE SMURFS AND THE BOOK THAT KNOWS EVERYTHING

Okay, I think I have everything: my grimoire, my notes, my toothsmurf, my hawthorn pills for blood pressure...

My young Smurfs, it's time for me to go! I have to be at Homnibus the Mage's home before nightfall.
Okay, Papa Smurf.

I don't know how long our research will go on... Whatever you do, don't smurf anything foolish during my absence. No magic, no chemistry experiments, no dangerous initiatives.
You can count on us, Papa Smurf.

And don't hesitate to alert me in case of an emergency! I'll come back as quickly as possible!
Yes, Papa Smurf.
Don't you smurf one bit!

Okay, I have to go. The stork is ready to leave.
Goodbye, Papa Smurf.
Bon voyage!

This trip worries me. Every time I go away, smurf goes awry!

I wonder why he stresses out like that when he smurfs on a trip...
You know, as you get older you worry over nothing.
1

Okay, see you later. I have a bunch of logs to smurf.

I feel like smurfing a nice surprise for Papa Smurf.

I'll go tidy up the laboratory a little. First, a nice smurf with the feather duster...

Sorry, you'll have to smurf another hiding place.

The Armoire of Forbidden Books... How careless leaving the key out. Someone might open it unknowingly.

Poor Papa Smurf, his trip really discomsmurfulated him. But now's my chance to smurf the dust out.

"Treatise on Black Magic"... "Lethal Poisons"... "Evil Spirits"... "The Book That Knows Everything"...

"The Book That Knows Everything"?... What smurfishness. There's no such book that knows everything.

But... if that book isn't for real, why did Papa Smurf smurf it in the armoire?

There's no harm in smurfing a quick, little look...

?

Oh, my!
FLAP
FLAP
FLAP

Unbelievable! There's nothing written in this book! Just the page numbers.

Let's smurf it another try. I'll open to the title page...
You may ask your question.

What was the water level yesterday at noon at the dam?
Water level of the dam: see page 87.

"The water level yesterday at noon: 79 cubits, 7 inches." It's true! I smurfed the measurement myself!

It's amazing! Awesome! This book is absolutely smurftastic!

What's gotten into you? Did you fall on your smurf?

Not at all, Hefty Smurf. I found a magic book... It speaks! And it answers questions! Come see for yourself.
Yeah, right! A talking book... That's a tall smurf!

Go ahead! Smurf to the title page and ask it a question.
Calm down there. Don't push me.

You may ask your question.
So, what are you waiting for? Speak!

Uh... what do I have to smurf to get even stronger?
How to increase one's muscle mass: see page 13.

It smurfed me the recipe for an ointment... I have to write it down.
You see? It knows everything! It's extraordinary!
4

I think I outdid myself this time!
Slurp!

Laboratory
MY CAKE!
SPROTCH
PAF
GAK!

Good job! What's got you smurfing around like a madman?
Sorry, but I'm in a hurry! It's because of the magic book that answers all questions.

You really did outdo yourself. It's delicious! Yum!
Every question? That's not possible!
Yes, every question!

I'd be interested if it could smurf me recipes.
I'm inshteshted, too.

Is it true about the book that answers everything?
Yes! I'm the one who found it.

So, I want to know how to smurf a soufflé that doesn't fall.
Get back, Greedy Smurf, you'll get it dirty!

?
That magic book is fantastic! I'm going to smurf this recipe right away!

5
A magic book? I'm curious to smurf that...
Let's go see.

Oh! Greedy Smurf, you're disgusting! At least, smurf properly.
It's not my fault! He smurfed me on the head because of that magic book that answers all questions.

That book there? I have a question to smurf!
Me too!
Okay, okay... but be quick.

The news soon spreads throughout the village...
Yes! A soufflé that never falls.
The book smurfed me the recipe for a toner that makes your hair silky and shiny.
It smurfed me a trick for always having a fresh, blue complexion.

I want to see that!
Let's smurf there quick before everybody knows about it.

Go on inside!
Smurf out of the way, I got here before you!
Oww! You're smurfing on my foot!
!

I want to know why Smurfs have tails.
And me, how to smurf rose bushes without thorns.
Where's my #12 wrench?
Why do I have hairs smurfing out my nose?
A rhyme with "My heart skips a beat."

...so, since he wanted some smurf, but didn't remember the word anymore, he said: "Pass me the... the smurf!"
6

So, that's the origin of the word! Nobody had ever told us.
Okay, are you about done?!

That's enough now! It's my turn!
Whoa! Calm down!

Your turn?! You sure have a lot of nerve!
Give it to me, or I'll smurf you a smack!
No! It's my turn!

ENOUGH!

Smurf me that book!

No way!
What's he smurfing?!

You're acting like a pack of smurfs! You're not worthy of this book!

Just whom do you smurf yourself for?
We want the book!
Smurf him down from there!
Back off!

I said: "BACK OFF!"
BIP
BAP
BOP

It's true... They'll end up ruining it!

I found the pipistrelle bat droppings. But where does one smurf some mandrake root?

I have to go back and smurf the book that question...
7

?
Get him down!
Smurf him off of there!
Go ahead, flip the table over!

What's smurfing on here? Move aside, you!

Stop right now! What's this circus?!

He took the book from us!
He's driving us smurf!
He thinks he can smurf us orders!
They're smurfing like savages! They'll end up tearing the pages out!

Brainy Smurf is right! We have to get organized! Stand in line! He'll hold the book while you smurf your question!
Okay, okay... fine!
If you say so...

Hey, Hefty Smurf, you got here after us! Get in line!
You want my fist in your smurf?

I want to ask it where mandrake root can be found!

I cannot answer your question for now. I have to recharge my energy.

See! You've exhausted it with all your stupid questions!
A book that has to rest. That's unsmurfed of.
Maybe, but it's a magic book.

Time to eat! The soufflé is smurfy!
DING
DILING
8

Oh, the lunch bell!
DING DILING DING
Perfect timing. I could smurf a horse.

Let's go eat. We'll come back afterwards.
There you have it! With them, their stomach smurfs before everything else.

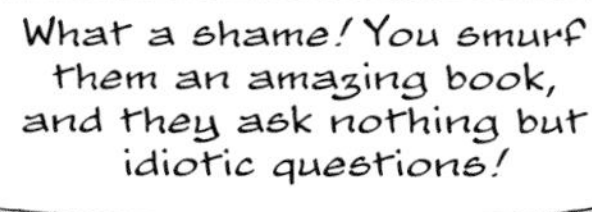
What a shame! You smurf them an amazing book, and they ask nothing but idiotic questions!

Once the book has recharged, they'll start over and exhaust it all over again. Someone intelligent and responsible will be needed to smurf good use of it...

It's clear: I must take it to my home!

How's the soufflé?
Smurfily good!
Delicious!
What will the main course be?
That's it, stuff yourselves!

I'd rather nourish my mind.

There, they'll smurf us in peace this way.
CLAK

Get some good rest.

Now I just have to wait until it resmurfs speech!
9

Ah, that was good!
Let's go see if that book is smurfing again.
Yes... I'd like it to smurf me a cure for smurfulence!
Chef Smurf, what do you think of my hair?
?

But... The book's not here!
Brainy Smurf neither! And he didn't come to eat...
That smurf in the grass took it with him!

That book is marvelous. I wonder why Papa Smurf has always smurfed its existence from us?

Why did Papa Smurf hide my existence: see page 112.
Oh! You're awake again!

He sure has a sense of entitlement!
It's time to smurf him in his place!

"Knowledge gives power. And Papa Smurf knows many things. But I know everything!"

That's true! He's Papa Smurf because he smurfs the solutions to all our problems... But with this book, we could do without him.

BOOM BOOM BOOM
What's that racket?!

It's already more shiny, don't you think?
Uh...
Brainy Smurf! Are you the one who smurfed the book? We want to ask it questions! Open the door!

No way! I'm the one who gets to decide when it can be used! Go away!
10

Smurfs, this is an abuse of power. The book belongs to everyone. We have to smurf it from him and use it smurfocratically.
Bravo, Poet Smurf!
Yeah, well smurfed!
Greedy Smurf?
No, it's me, Vanity Smurf. This is a mask that smurfs a fresh complexion.

What does "smurfocratically" mean?
Uh... it's a little hard to exsmurf! Ask the book...

Action must be taken! I'll smash the door open in the name of the Smurf people!
Yeah! Go for it, Hefty Smurf!

CRASH

I... really... need to smurf that... ointment... that develops... muscles!

No worries. We'll smurf the door down with a battering ram...

They've gotten violent. They're going to smurf the book from me!

Only you can smurf me a solution! I want to keep you for myself!
How to keep others from using me: see page 88.
11

Forward, Smurfs!
We'll smurf it into pieces!

"Recognize and answer only me!" That's all I have to say? Cool!

Quick! Those brutes are going to smurf my door!
BOOM

We got it this time!
Charge!

You knocked?
?!

CRAK
BOOM
BAM
BING
OWW!

Is this the book you wanted? Here you go!
?

You're right not to resist! That'll keep me from smurfing you some smacks!
Yes, right! Here.

Let's try it out!
Yes, let's see if it's smurfing again.
Me, first! I have to find out where mandrake root can be found!

Please identify yourself!
12

What's gotten into it?! It's never smurfed that before!
Answer! Tell it who you are.

Uh... I'm Hefty Smurf!
Sorry, access denied.

Whatever! This book is smurfing me!
Smurf it to me!

Please identify yourself.
I'm Handy Smurf!

Sorry, access denied.
Ah! You see?
Let me try.

Hello, nice book. It's me, Smurfette.

Sorry, access denied.
Oh! You ill-mannered smurf of a book!

What's going on?
We can no longer smurf it a question!
Really? Give it to me, and I'll show you...

Please identify yourself.
It's me... Brainy Smurf.

You may ask your question.
Thanks, I don't need you for the moment!

But... what's the meaning of this?
That the book has recognized me as its caretaker and will only smurf me now.
13

He's got us this time.
We really are at his mercy.
There's no use in smurfing the book from him.

Wait, I have an idea!

Would you smurf me the book... and your glasses, too?
Uh... If you want, Jokey Smurf...

Please identify yourself.
It's me... BRAINY SMURF.

Sorry, access denied.
Well, smurf!
Good try, Jokey Smurf! Now, give me back the book... and my glasses!

Don't feel bad, I'll take the high road. I'll smurf you access to the book... if you behave yourselves.

Right now, I'm hungry. Is there any soufflé left?
No, they smurfed all of it.

But I can smurf a new one just for you.
Thanks, Chef Smurf!

Aren't you ashamed?
You're smurfing his boots!
Smurf-noser!
Me, I don't like smurf-nosers!
14

That was very good, Chef Smurf.
Thanks for smurfing the book my question.

Starting tomorrow, I'll smurf one of these nutritious, ten-minute recipes.
They'll probably turn out really good. The book is never wrong.

When can we smurf the book our questions?
Not now! I'm going to smurf an after-dinner walk first.

I'm not out of the woods yet... My situation is going to get difficult.

They're not going to leave me alone anymore... I can already picture them gathering outside my door from morning till night smurfing me crazy with their questions.

Maybe I should move to a more secluded place... But where?

That's a question to smurf the book!

Please identify yourself.
It's me, your caretaker, Learned Smurf!

Sorry, access denied.

Oh, all right, it's me Brainy smurf! You didn't recognize me?
Yes, but that's no reason for talking nonsense. Now, you may ask your question.
15

The old tower... The book smurfed correctly, like always.

I can isolate myself up there. They won't come smurfing their noses in my windows...

They'll wait in front of the door, and I'll only let them come up one by one...

BOOOM

Obviously there's a little repair work to be smurfed.

Bah! Handy Smurf will take care of it! He can't say no to that!
TAP TAP

He wants to move to the old tower. He asked me to smurf him a new door there and a new staircase.

You have to say no! If we start giving into all of his whims, we're smurfed!
You're right, Hefty Smurf!
He can go smurf in the lake!
Me, I don't like lakes.
16

The next morning...
Hello, Farmer Smurf! Do you think it'll be nice out?
If we had the book, it'd tell us the answer.

TCHIRK TCHIRK TCHIRK
?

Hello, Handy Smurf. Where are you smurfing with all those boards?
TCHIRK TCHIRK TCHIRK

If Brainy Smurf moves into the old tower, I have to smurf a new staircase there. It's a matter... uh... of safety.

Safety, my eye!
Another one who's going to become his pet. And he'll be able to smurf the book lots of questions.
TCHIRK TCHIRK TCHIRK

Wait for us, Handy Smurf!
We're going to smurf those stairs with you!
TCHIRK TCHIRK TCHIRK

And now they're all smurfing his game! It's pathetic!

Hello, Hefty Smurf.
Oh! You were there!

Say, did you ever find that mandrake root for your ointment?
No! I have no idea where it grows.
17

If you want, we could ask the book...
Oh! Really?

Of course! Come, let's go inside your home where nobody will bother us.

Say, will you help me with my move? With the ointment, it'll be child's smurf for you!
Uh... Okay.

The work is efficiently carried out...

Mean-while...
Just passing by... for an ordinary, little root...
EEEK

So, what do you smurf about that?
You smurfed good work. But there's still one problem...

The book must be smurfed very dry. I should hang draperies in the room.

Draperies?
We'll have to ask Tailor Smurf for fabric...
Oh, yes, one other thing. I'll need help for consultations.

Dopey Smurf, do you want to be my assistant?
Me? Uh... sure!

Dopey Smurf? What an idea!
He's clueless!
He really doesn't smurf his left hand from his right!
He's exactly the Smurf I need! Obedient and none too sharp.
18

Here! This is the last one.
It won't be enough. We'll have to smurf some elsewhere.

Smurfette, uh... do you have a few extra bedsheets?
Hold on, I'm finish-ing my hairdo.

Your hair really is shiny!
Isn't it? It's thanks to the book's toner.

And me? Did you see how fresh my complexion is?
Meh! Nobody smurfs about your complexion.

Hefty Smurf! You're not going to smurf the move all by yourself?!
Why not? The ointment has made me as strong as a smurf!

My friends, I am very satisfied! You know, deep down, I have very simple tastes.

To thank you, I'll let you smurf the book your questions tomorrow morning.

Hurray!
Hurray for Brainy Smurf!
Hey, now! Don't get too smurfed away.
19

Early that morning, at Lazy Smurf's...
SNRR ZZZZZ

DRIIING

The sun is up. I have to go smurf the book my question.

If I get there first, I won't have to wait... and then I can smurf back to bed!

Uh... Good morning, Lazy Smurf. Where are you smurfing so early?
To the tower... and you?
Oh? Me, too.

Oh, my smurfness!
What a bunch of smurfs!

Don't tell me they have an important question to smurf, too!
And what's yours?

I want it to give me a cure for insomnia.
You have insomnia?!

No! But if that happened to me, it would be awful. Just the idea smurfs me nightmares...
20

The consultations are getting started!
Aaah!
At last!
None too soon!
Z

Next!
Z
Lazy Smurf, move ahead!

Sorry, but you'll have to wait! The book has to resmurf its energy!
Oooooh!

Z

Okay, the consultations will start again!
Aaaaah!

Lazy Smurf, move ahead! It's your turn!
Z

You can go up, Lazy Smurf.

For smurf's sake! It's high!

These stairs are exsmurfing! Aren't they, Dopey Smurf?

You're telling me?! This is the twenty-fifth time I've smurfed up it this morning... ->Pfff!<- ...Assistant work is hard!

L... ->pfff!<- ...Lazy Smurf... ->Pfff!<-...
Let him in!
21

!

Oh! You're wearing a nightshirt?!
No! I told you: it gets cold in this tower!

Yes, but your cap... How do you go to bed?
It's NOT a nightcap, it keeps the spiders from smurfing on my nose! Do you want to ask your question or not?!

We're listening!
You may ask your question.

So, did you get a cure for insomnia?
Yes, some plant-based thing...

But, between us... I think he's getting a little smurfy.
Meh! So long as he lets us ask our questions...

Everything changes very quickly in the village...
The meal isn't ready yet?
No! The book just smurfed me the recipe.
I don't have time to sharpen it right now. I have to go smurf the book a question.
GONE TO THE TOWER.
28

The mole that was smurfing holes in my lawn is gone. The trick the book gave me smurfed wonderfully.

Oh, you think so? It's in my yard now!
Sorry! Everybody has problems.

And that's true. Let him go smurf in line at the tower like me.

AAAH!

Potter Smurf? Have you lost your smurf?
Not at all.

The book told me I'd find the best potter's clay in your yard. And it's true!

You idiot! Go smurf your dirt elsewhere!
You selfish smurf! Don't come smurfing to me when you need a jar!
Oh, my! There they go quarreling again like little smurfs!

AHHH! MY ROSEBUSHES!

Vanity Smurf! Have you gone crazy?!
No, let me explain.
23

The book gave me a formula for an ointment that hides wrinkles around your eyes.

And that's why you hacked down my lovely garden?!
You need lots and lots of fresh roses... but I'll smurf you a jar of ointment.

You monster! My beautiful roses! And I **DON'T** have wrinkles around my eyes either!
Oww! Ouch!

I'm covered with scratches! They sting!
Ask the book for a cure!
Whoa! Things have smurfed between Smurfette and Vanity Smurf!

Hey... What's that smurfy odor?
SNIF SNIF

>Sniff!<... >sniff!<... It's smurfing from here!

Painter Smurf... What are you smurfing?
Smurf blue paint. The book gave me a recipe for smurfing it in large quantities.

Look! The tint is perfect!
Yesh, but it'sh shburfing up the whole neighborhood!

Bah! I'll ask the book to smurf me an air freshener.
24

Meanwhile, at the tower...
Flighty Smurf, it's your turn!

FLIGHTY SMURF!
Oh! Coming!

Fli...pfff...
Flighty Smurf...
Let him in!

You may ask your question.
Go ahead.

So, I...

I'd like to know... uh...

One moment, I... I've forgotten my question...
Any day now?!

I'm still awaiting your question.

Okay, come back some other time. We have no time to smurf!
Oh, no, please! It'll smurf back to me in a moment or so...

Next!
That's so dumb. I smurfed in line all morning long.

That happens to me all the time. I should smurf something about it...

For smurf's sake! That's what I wanted to ask the book... A method for smurfing my memory!
25

You may ask your question.
I'd like to know...

...what I should do for Smurfette to love me!
Hey! I don't like that kind of question!

How to be loved by Smurfette: see page 138.
Come on, don't be smurfing, let me read the answer!

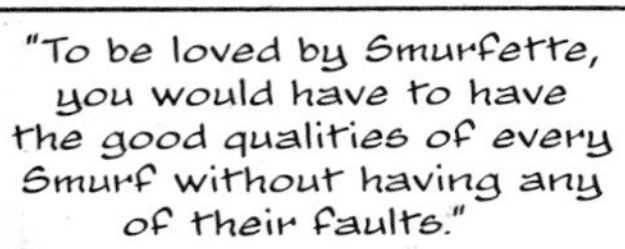
"To be loved by Smurfette, you would have to have the good qualities of every Smurf without having any of their faults."

What an answer! That got me nowhere!
That'll teach you! I won't let anyone ask questions about Smurfette!

They're over the top! For their own good, I'll have to start screening the questions.

Besides, if Smurfette were to love anyone, it would be me, for my intelligence!

Brainy Smurf...
Yes, Dopey Smurf. You didn't smurf the next one up?

No! I'd like to smurf a question myself, please.

A question, you? Sure... if you want.

I'm so tired of smurfing up those stairs... I'd like to know if there's a way to make it easier.
Solution so that Dopey Smurf will be less tired: see page 53.

"Brainy Smurf and Dopey Smurf simply have to trade jobs from time to time."
26

Ha! Ha! Ha! Good one! That book sure has a sense of humor!

But... I thought it was always right.
Of course! But here, it smurfed a little joke to relax some.

All right, go get one last Smurf. Then I'll stop for today.

You can... ⇒pfff⇐ ...go up... J... Jokey Smurf...
Uh oh! The assistant isn't looking so good!

It's you? I hope you have a serious question to ask.
Of course!

You may ask your question.
Tell me... How can I ask you a question without Brainy Smurf being nosy?

TRAITOR! HOW DARE YOU?!
CLAP

Come on, it was a joke! I'm going to smurf another question!
Definitely not! Get out of here right now!

This is outrageous! We can't laugh anymore?
That wasn't funny! You're denied any consultations till further notice!

He's restricting me from returning over a little joke... Who does that tyrant think he is?!
27

Bah! He doesn't need to smurf those idiotic jokes.
And that'll make one less Smurf in line.
The ones smurfing stupid questions really are wasting our time.
Yes. Starting with you.

Consultations are over for today.

What?!
Then we've been smurfing in line for nothing?
That's just wrong!

You'll come back tomorrow, that's all! And I'm warning you: you'll have to submit your question to me before smurfing it to the book.

He really is over the top!
He's abusing his power!
Yes, but without him, we're smurfed.

What are we smurfing today?
Lentil soup!

Again!
Lentil soup is very healthy. The book said so.

I've come to get Brainy Smurf's meal.
I smurfed a light dish for him... puff pastries with mushrooms.

And I'd like a chunk of that big melon for dessert.
That's a pumpkin, Dopey Smurf.

28
Puff pastry with mushroom... And we get smurfed lentil soup!
That does it!
→Psst!← Smurf down!
Yes! Dopey might repeat to him what you're all saying.

And, the next day...
Are you going to the tower?
Yes, I have a good question smurfing around in my head!

I hope the weather will be nice. That's more pleasant while smurfing in line.

Hello, Farmer Smurf. Are you going to the field?
No. I have to ask the book the best date for planting carrots.

Me,I don't like standing in line at the tower.

But I HATE being the only one who doesn't smurf the book questions.

Arrooo!
No, Baby Smurf, not you. You're too little.

What? Smurfette hasn't opened her shutters.
Vanity Smurf either!

A little later...
Thanks for the ride. See you next time.

This trip has been exhausting... I hope everything has smurfed well in the village.
23

Wow! Farmer Smurf has neglected his garden... He must be sick...

And this one smurfed a hole in his lawn. And he used to smurf after his yard like crazy...

What? The laboratory door is open?!

Someone has taken my things! What have they smurfed now?!

Okay, we'll see about that later! I'm smurfing of hunger!
GROUIIIK

Chef Smurf?

Nobody! But he should be smurfing the meal by now.

Everything is poorly smurfed! And nobody is around!

Ah! Perfect timing! Tell me--
Oh, hello, Papa Smurf! Are you back already?

One moment, there's something I'd like to try right away...
30

I'm hallucinating! They've gone crazy!
CLOSED

Oh! Smurfette's rosebushes have been completely hacked down!

Boo-hoo-hoo!
Smurfette!

Papa Smurf, are you back?
What's happened? Wait, I'm coming!

I don't want anyone to see me... I look awful!
Oh, my, what are you smurfing me? Open up, come now!

Oh! Uh... you colored your hair?

No, I wanted it to be shiny and silky! I used the toner...
What toner?

It's a formula from the Book that Knows Everything!
THE BOOK THAT KNOWS EVERYTHING? For smurf's sake! Who took it?

Brainy Smurf!
I knew some smurftastrophe would happen! I had a bad feeling!

Papa Smurf?
AAAH!
31

It's me, Papa Smurf... Vanity Smurf!
You smurfed me a shock! What's happened to you?
BODOM BOM BODOM

I wanted to have a fresh complexion, and the book smurfed me an ointment... Now my complexion is fresh but I have horrible pimples!

You see, that book is very dangerous! It gives answers for everything, without warning of the consequences! If you smurf everything it says, it'll always end badly!

I must get it back! Where is Brainy Smurf?
In the old tower...
That's where he smurfs his consultations.

His consultations! That takes the cake!

He's going to have to deal with me! I'm going to smurf him an earful!

Hey, Papa Smurf is back.
He doesn't look happy.
No. And he looks ill.

Let me by, Dopey Smurf! I have to talk with Brainy Smurf!

Uh... I don't know if I can... It's not your turn.
That's right, Papa Smurf, you have to smurf in line.

SMURF IN LINE, ME?!
32

Let him smurf up! I'll see him!

That's fine, Papa Smurf, you can--uh...

Wow! He still smurfs fast at his age!

Pa... Papa... ->pfff!<-... Papa Smurf!

All right then! What is this farce?
Calm down, Papa Smurf!

Sit down, you must be tired...

I'd rather stand! Who said you could take that book?!
I found it by chance while smurfing the dusting.

Papa Smurf, you shouldn't have hidden the existence of that wonderful book from us!

That book is very dangerous! It smurfs disasters and causes conflict!

Papa Smurf, I understand that you're afraid of losing power... after all these years!

Don't be scared, we'll continue to respect your wisdom and great experience... But the book's knowledge must be smurfed available to everyone.
33

Enough smurfing! I'm taking the book back!
No way! Over my dead smurf!

Dopey Smurf, you show Papa Smurf out! This conversation is over!

That's fine, I'll leave you to your illusions. He who smurfs last, smurfs best!

Listen up! Brainy Smurf has smurfed his sense of reality. He refuses to admit the book is dangerous.

Go home! Nobody is to smurf here anymore! He'll eventually come to his senses once we no longer pay him any mind.

But, Papa Smurf, we can't do without it.
We still have lots of questions to smurf the book.
For real, it's smurfily practical.
Now that we've smurfed it, we can't do without it.

OH, FOR SMURF'S SAKE! YOU MAKE ME MAD!

Oh... I... I don't feel well!

Papa Smurf?
34

What's going on?
Papa Smurf has fainted!

I'll ask the book for advice! Come back up, Dopey Smurf!

Don't worry, Papa Smurf, we'll soon know what we must do.

Here... instructions... from... the... book...

I already feel better...
No, Papa Smurf, you're exhausted!
We're going to take you home and smurf you to bed.

I promise you, I'm okay! It was just a dizzy spell.
No, no! The book said you should smurf some rest.

I'm thirsty.
Here, drink this.

That's good. Smurf all of it.

This smurfonade has a funny taste.

Oh, my! I'm... sleepy...
He'll sleep well! That's the cure for insomnia that the book smurfed to Lazy Smurf!
35

Much later...
Oh, my head! What happened?

I remember! The Book that Knows Everything, Brainy Smurf... What a mess!

Before anything else, I have to resmurf my strength. I have to eat.

For smurf's sake! They've locked me in! They've gone totally smurf!

Hey! I want to smurf out of here right now, do you hear me?!

Papa Smurf! Are you feeling better?

Yes, but I'm hungry and the door is smurfed! Let me out of here!
Uh... How? We don't have the key...

Call Handy Smurf... Or Hefty Smurf, so he can break down the door!
Handy Smurf is still at the tower! And I don't know where Hefty Smurf--

Here I am, Papa Smurf!

Hefty Smurf! What's wrong with you?
The book smurfed me an ointment, and I became smurfily strong...

But now, I hurt all over. I can barely walk...
Another harmful effect of the book.
38

Well, I'll just have to smurf out through the window.

Smurf heavens, I'm too old for this. Help me.

Quick! To the dining hall. I'll eat whatever I can find...

Oh! Papa Smurf got out!
The book said he was supposed to rest!

And I'm telling you I'm fine and I simply have to eat.
But... The book is always right!

Always right?! My tail!

Look at the color of my hair!
And I have lots of pimples!
I can barely walk!
You made mistakes while smurfing the mixtures, that's all.
If you're too dumb to read a recipe, too bad for you!
?

Too dumb? I still have enough strength to smurf you a thrashing!
I'd like to see that.

STOP!
37

There's no use fighting! If you want to trust that book, I accept it!

But I don't want to see it. I'd rather smurf my distance... I'm going to move to the cave on Mount Smurf.

If you need me again, you know where to smurf me!

Come on, Papa Smurf, you can't abandon us.
I'm not abandoning you.

But I can't convince them they're mistaken. They have to figure it out on their own.

While I wait for them to see things more clearly, I'll stay up there. I'm going to work on your little problems...
Oh, thanks, Papa Smurf! I can't stand being so ugly!

You see, I'll be just fine here.
¿

There... you're prettier like that!
Papa Smurf, what if we stayed with you?
No! You should go back to the village and keep me informed about what's smurfing... Don't worry, everything will end up smurfing back to normal.

At least I hope so!

The next morning...
➛Yawn!⬸ ...I slept well. I needed that!

Smurfette.... You're already back?
I smurfed you your breakfast.

So, what's the story in the village?
It seems they all have bad stomach aches.

It's probably because of the cabbage soup they ate yesterday! Luckily, I don't eat in the dining hall anymore!

But cabbage soup is good.
Yes, but Farmer Smurf had treated them with an anti-slug product.

One smurfed by the book?
Of course! Some sugar for your sarsaparilla tea?

They're not ready to open their eyes, Smurfette... But they will.

Meanwhile, let's think about your hair... And also about Vanity Smurf and Handy Smurf.

I'm going to smurf some plants to fix all that.
I'm going home. I have to look after Baby Smurf. See you soon.

Besides that, I'll also need some arnica for Hefty Smurf's stiffness...

Okay, with this handful of maidenhair fern, I have everything I need.

Papa Smurf! Come quick!
What's happened now?

It's Painter Smurf! He's very sick... He has a smurfing fever!
Blue... blue... it all looks blue...

He mixed a new Smurf blue color...
...from a formula from the book. And now he's pale blue.

It smelled smurfily bad... He must be poisoned!
Okay. He'll stay here. The fresh air will do him good.

Papa Smurf, I'd like to smurf here with him. I'll take care of him when you leave.

Excellent idea! That's a very smurfy gesture on your part.
Uh... There's another reason.

Since that smell was smurfing up my whole house, I asked the book for an air-freshener...

Now it's that smell that smurfing me nauseous!
Well, welcome to the cave. You both need fresh air.

Blue... blue... when it's gray, I smurf blue!
Do you think he'll get better, Papa Smurf?
Yes... But what does that book still have in store for us?

What nasty weather.
Yes, it rained all night.

But I have to go smurf some plants to treat him. His fever hasn't gone down.
Blue... blue... the sky is blue...

Hey! Where can that cracking sound be smurfing from?
CRRRR
CRRRR

The dam! It's about to break!

I bet nobody has checked the water level since my departure!

And nobody has opened the sluice gate... they were too busy with that book!

This won't be enough! The level of the lake is going to smurf more with this rain!

I need help to avoid a smurftastrophe!
41

There's no use going to the village! I'll smurf most of them at the tower!

Smurfs! Come quick!

Because of your carelessness, the dam is going to give way! We have to smurf a breach in it so the water flows out faster!

Follow me, we have to smurf axes!

What... They're obeying him!? They're all leaving!

Is everyone equipped?
Yes, Papa Smurf!

Quick, to the dam!

Wait! Where are you all smurfing like that?
42

The dam is going to smurf.
We're going to smurf a big hole it so the water can empty out.

Calm down! How do you know it's going to smurf? That's not certain!

Stop your smurflishness! It's obvious it's about to give way!

No, we have to ask the book! Why damage the dam unnecessarily?

That's right! If we smurf a hole in the dam, we'll have to repair it!
Ask the book, it'll only smurf a few seconds!

Good! I'll smurf it the question...

Sorry, I still need a few moments to recharge my energy.

Enough wasting time! Let's go!
NO! It'll answer in a minute!

43
We'd better go!
No, let's wait a bit.
What if the dam smurfs?
It'll surely hold out a minute longer.
Frankly, I don't know what to smurf anymore.
The book will tell us!

CRRRAAAC

It gave way!
Smurf for your lives!

Of course not, come on! Smurf here, it's just a storm!

!

The book! I have to smurf it out of the water! -Glub!-...

Papa Smurf, will the water smurf our village?
I don't think so! But we'd better evacuate!

Is everyone here? Let's smurf towards the hill!
Papa Smurf! It's terrible!

Baby Smurf isn't in the house! I can't smurf him anywhere! I don't know where he could have gone!

Smurf heavens! If he followed us along the river, he may get smurfed by the flood!
44

Aroo
aroo!
?

You poor thing! What are you smurfing here?!

The water is rising! We have to smurf away from here! But how do I swim with the book and you?

Papa Smurf! He's there on a rock with Brainy Smurf!

Book, smurf an effort... Tell me what I must do!
Answer: page 1.

"It's impossible to save both of us. Since I'm the most important thing in the world, you must--
Ga...

"...abandon Baby Smurf!"

Aroo... Hee hee!
?

But... But... You're a monster!
?

45
There! If you're so smart, smurf yourself on your own!

OH! He... he smurfed the book in the water!
He's carrying Baby Smurf!

Brainy Smurf! This way!
Smurf onto the branch!

There! They're smurfed! Everything is okay!

Papa Smurf, it's awful! That horrible book wanted me to abandon Baby Smurf... So I smurfed it into the river.

That book is extraordinary but smurfily dangerous too. Its power makes you lose your mind. That's why I kept it hidden.

But you smurfed the right decision. Let's forget the rest.
Yes, Papa Smurf will take care of us and everything will smurf back to normal.
Take my cap, it's dry. You might smurf a head cold.

Still, it's too bad. A book that smurfs the answer to everything was useful.

I have an idea. I'll write a huge ensmurfopedia that collects all the knowledge of the Smurfs!

END

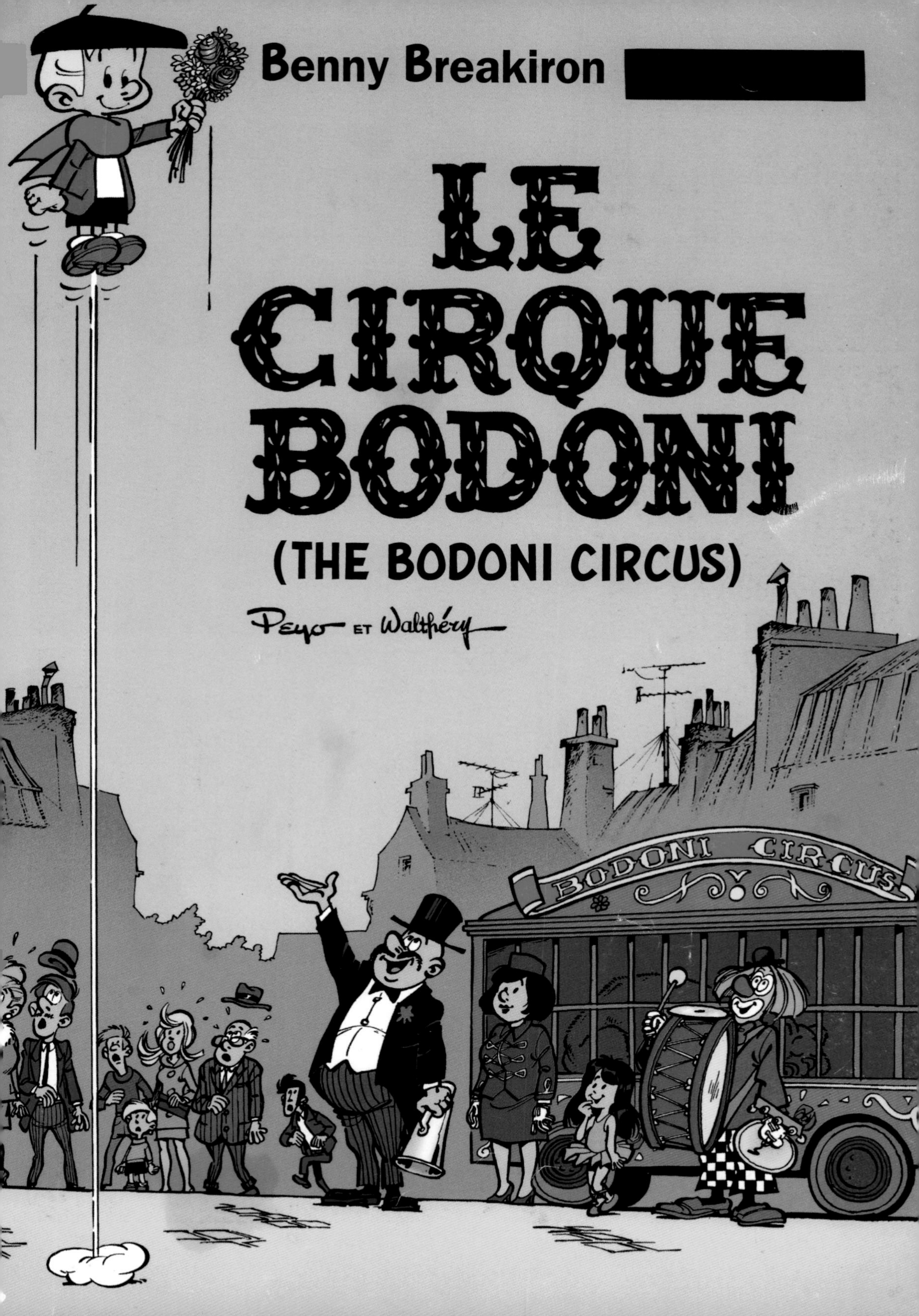
Benny Breakiron
LE CIRQUE BODONI
(THE BODONI CIRCUS)
Peyo ET Walthéry
BODONI CIRCUS

One day in Vivejoie-la-Grande in the Jules Petty Square...

Pow! Good one, Louis!

TCHIC

UNIQUE, SENSATIONAL, INTERNATIONALLY FAMOUS CROWD PLEASERS! SEE YOU TONIGHT AT EIGHT!

A few hours later...
The Gourmet Clown

BLING BILING BING
GOLDEN Hazelnut Chocolate Bar

I'm sorry, young lady, but you don't have enough money for a chocolate.
KWA KWA The Good Chocolate

Goodbye, ma'am!
Hey! That's the girl from the circus!

And what would you like, Benny?
A chocolate hazelnut bar!

Goodbye, Madame Cuberdon!

Hey, do you want half of my candy bar?
Oh, yes! Thanks! You're nice!
EGG

Want me to carry your bag?
Sure! But I'm warning you, it's very heavy.

Maybe, but I'm really strong. But you mustn't tell anybody.

Hey, I recognize you! You were riding the horse this morning in the circus parade.
Yes! My name is Mona. And you?
Benny!

My brother's name is Pietro. He was the clown. My dad was the ringmaster. And Mama was there too. We all do a bunch of show numbers.

It must be a lot of fun living in a circus. I'd really like that.
Oh! You know, it's not fun all the time. Especially since we're not well off.

You go to bed late. You have to get up early. You're in a different town every day. So I never have any friends.

AZA CAFÉ
So! Here we are.
B
BODONI
BODONI

Thanks for the bag and the chocolate. Will you come see the show tonight?
Yes, of course.

I'm sorry, but if you don't pay today, I'll have to foreclose! This is your final deadline!

But I'm telling you I don't have the money right now.
I get it, Mr. Bodoni, but what can I say? I have to do my job.

Wait at least until tonight. I can pay you after the show.
Okay. See you then.

What a job! Oh! If I hadn't listened to my father, I'd have followed my calling and became a packinghouse slaughterer.
Are they going to sell the circus, Daddy?
I don't think so. At least, I hope not.

You know what I'm going to do? I'll tell all my friends to come tonight. That way, there'll be lots of people, and you'll have lots of money.

That'd be really very nice, young man.

Count on me. There'll be a crowd. See you tonight, Mona.

Hey! Chris!

Did you see? There's a circus in Market Square! It's awesome! You totally have to come see the show tonight!

You're crazy! There's an episode of "Doctor Who" on TV tonight. Now, that's a show.
But... the circus is fun and--

Nope, no way, buddy. All right, bye, have fun anyhow.

Go to the circus? I'd like to, but I'm grounded. This morning I broke a window with my ball.

It's not possible, little Benny! Joey is in bed. He has the flu.

ABSOLUTELY NOT! You already went to the movies yesterday!
But, Dad!

Uh, no. Some friends invited my parents over, and I have to babysit my little brother.

To the circus? You're not thinking, Benny. I have math homework this evening.

Sure. Good idea. Okay. See you tonight.
AVEC
BEAUTY

And that evening...
I'm late! I hope there's still room.

Hey! Benny! Over here!
!

One ticket, please.
TICKETS

GOOD EVENING, LADIES AND GENTLEMEN! OUR BIG SHOW FOR TONIGHT WILL OPEN WITH AN ASTONISHING ACROBATICS NUMBER ON HORSEBACK...

...PERFORMED BY OUR YOUNG RIDER, MISS MONA!... MISS MONA!

I know her. She's nice. I met her this afternoon.
Oh?

It's awesome, isn't it? What do you think?
CLAP
CLAP
Meh!

HURRAY! HURRAY!
CLAP
CLAP CLAP
CLAP CLAP
CLAP CLAP
CLAP

Hmm, hmm... and here now, performed by myself, Beethoven's 5th Symphony!

Oh. I know that number. You'll see, there's a clown who's going to want to play and, since the other one says no, he puts a firecracker inside the piano and it blows up. It's dumb.

Hey, Mr. Chouvert, may I play the piano?
No way! Out of the question, Mr. Augustus. Go away!

You don't really mean that?
Nope!
Not even a little?
NO!
Too bad, you'll regret it.

Please excuse this ridiculous interruption. So now, ladies and gentlemen, Beethoven's 5th Symphony!

BANG

See? I told you so.
Oh! Look, a juggler!

=Pff!=
Yeah! Not so great, eh?

I've seen better on TV!
Don't complain. You're the one who wanted to come.
RRR
ZZZ
8

An hour later...
Boring!
That was awful!
We should've gone to the movies.
BODONI CIRCUS

Okay, buddy, you got me with your circus. No hard feelings. Bye.
But it wasn't that bad. I liked it.

Hey, there's Monsieur Bodoni! He's settling his debts with the banker.

That's perfect, it's all accounted for. But good heavens, you don't have anything left!
Well, no.

I'm sorry, Monsieur Bodoni. I did my best to bring my friends, but I wasn't very lucky.
It's okay, you're very kind to try.

I saw you give him all your money. How will you eat tomorrow?
Bah! We'll manage.

All right, don't worry about us anymore. It's getting late. Get to bed soon!
Oui! Goodnight, Monsieur Bodoni.

Those poor people. Mona won't be buying herself any chocolate soon.

I ought to do something to help them! But what?...

But you can't force people to go to the circus! If only I... I-- ZZZ... ZZZ...

The next morning...

CLINC
CLINC

CRAC

Sapristi! What have I done now?

Six fifty plus eighty-four cents makes seven thirty-four! And...

It's not much, but that'll let them eat today.

?!

The circus? Oh! It left really early this morning, kid. I heard they were going eighteen miles from here. To Mangetout.
10

A few hours later, in Mangetout...

YOOHOO! MONA!

Benny! Oh, wow! What are you doing here?

Well, uh... here! I brought you my piggybank savings.
Oh! Benny!

We really can't take this, Benny.

Now, please excuse us, but we're about to raise the big top. Thanks again.

Hey, I'd really like to be able to do some performances like you all. Is it hard?
Oh, no. Do you want to try?

Here! First you'll learn how to juggle. Throw them in the air one after the other and catch them as they fall one by one. Go ahead.

BOP
BOP
Hee-hee! Hee-hee!

Try this.
It's not as
hard.

All right!
Keep going!
That's it...
you got it!

NO!
LOOK OUT!
YOU'RE--

Poor Benny. You
really don't have
a knack for this
kind of thing.
BAP

The hoist is broken.
We'll have to raise
the tent by hand!

Heave-ho! Heave-ho!
No! Stop, we'll
never make it!

May
I help,
Monsieur
Bodoni?
Who?
You?

Sure!
Ha! Ha! Ha!
Here, pull
hard!

FLOP
!?
!
12

A bit later...
...ITS JUGGLERS, IT'S DANCING BEAR...
You think so?
Yes, it will! You'll see!

...AND IN THE STARRING ACT, A UNIQUE, UNBELIEVABLE, SENSATIONAL ATTRACTION...

BENNY! THE STRONGEST LITTLE BOY IN THE WORLD!

BENNY CAN LIFT THE HEAVIEST WEIGHTS!

Oh, yeah? Well, let him lift the fallen soldiers monument.. Now that's heavy! Ha! Ha! Ha!

Come on, there's no reason to exaggerate. Benny isn't--
No, no! Let me, Monsieur Bodoni.

?
!
OH!
!
OH!
!

NOT ONLY IS BENNY SUPER STRONG, HE ALSO RUNS SUPER FAST! READY, BENNY? ONE... TWO... THREE... GO!

THERE YOU HAVE IT, LADIES AND GENTLE-MEN, A LAP AROUND THE SQUARE IN THREE POINT TWO SECONDS! WHO CAN TOP THAT?

And that's not all! Benny can jump super high! He's going to give these flowers to that lady there on the fifth floor!

Here you go, madame!

Did you see that? It's... it's incredible!
Oh, yes! That's the first time anybody's given me flowers in thirty years.

Isn't it fantastic?
Yes, we can't miss a show like that.
AN AFTERNOON PERFORMANCE AND TONIGHT AT EIGHT, EVERYBODY COME SEE A ONE-OF-A-KIND SHOW PUT ON BY THE BODONI CIRCUS!

You were wonderful, Benny! Thanks to you, there'll definitely be a crowd later.

That afternoon...
I'm sorry, but there's not a single seat left! And the show has already begun, too, but you can get a ticket for tonight!
YAY!
AGAIN!
AGAIN!
TICKETS

AND NOW, HERE ARE OUR CLOWNS, GUS AND ROCKY!
CLAP CLAP
CLAP
AGAIN!
CLAP
CLAP
AGAIN!
CLAP

HELLO, KIDS! HELLO, HELLO!

Oh! Mister Gus? Why the crossbow? I thought we were going to play some music?
That's right. It's to play the William Tell Overture! Let's do it!

presto agitato
PLMM
PLAMPLMM
PLMM

Hey, Monsieur Gus, you're making a mistake! That's not how William Tell used his crossbow!
Oh! No? How did he use it then?

It's real simple! He shot an arrow into an apple set on his son's head! Give me your crossbow and go find an apple! I'll show you!

An apple? Oh. Okay.

Here you go!
HA! HA! HA!
HA! HA! HA! HA!
15

Really? Your apple is way too big!

Ringmaster, throw me an apple, please! A real one!

Merci!

All right! One of you, go stand on the other side of the ring!
Uh... it's... it's getting late! I got to go home!
Me, too! I suddenly remember leaving soup on the stove!

Is there a volunteer in the room? No? Well, too bad! I'll do this number all by myself, then!

TCHAC

TCHOC

CLAP
BRAVO!
Unbelievable! This act is awesome!
CLAP
CLAP
CLAP
AGAIN!

I have to call the boss!

Hello, boss? It's Leon on the line! Jump in your car and head over to Mangetout to the Bodoni Circus! There's a show number that'll interest you. I got you a ticket for tonight's show.
TELEPHONE

Benny's success in the evening equals that of the afternoon...
BRAVO!
AGAIN!
AGAIN!
CLAP
CLAP

CLAP
CLAP
CLAP
CLAP
CLAP
CLAP

So? What did I tell you, boss?
Yeah! You were right! He's fantastic!

AND NOW, LADIES AND GENTLEMEN, HERE ARE THE FAMOUS PIETRO AND MONA IN THEIR HIGH-FLYING ACT!

AA!
EEEE!

AAAH!

Hup!

CLAP
AGAIN! AGAIN!
HURRAY!
CLAP CLAP
CLAP CLAP
CLAP
CLAP
CLAP

Whew! I really thought he'd miss her.
Me too! That kid's awesome! I absolutely have to have him!
17

And the show ends to thunderous applause.

I'm glad I came!
Benny's awesome, isn't he, Dad?
There's surely some trick, but it's well done.

Good job, Benny! You were fantastic!
Look at this box office, everyone! We'll have to buy a new cigar box. This one really is too small.

Oh! You're wonderful, Benny! I have to give you a kiss!

We're going to celebrate this! Go get us a nice bottle, Pietro!
Some bubbly?

NO! CHAMPAGNE!

Meanwhile, I'll go put our earnings in safekeeping.

Hello, Bodoni!

Mr. Choesels! That's who you are, aren't you?
In person!

Choesels of Choesels Circuses. Five big tops. The biggest menageries. All the world famous attractions. More than six hundred employees. Offices around the world. It's all me.

Bodoni, the number with young Benny ain't bad. He intrigues me. I'll buy his contract out. How much?

He doesn't have a contract! He's a nice kid who did that to help us out, and I don't know if--

No contract? Ha! Ha! Ha! Imbecile!

Where's the kid?
In the tent! Uh... Surely you're not going to--

Hey, kid! I'm Choesels, the head of Choesels Circuses!
Bonjour, monsieur!

Your show number's not bad. But with the resources at my disposal, it could be better. Well, we'll see about that later.

Look. I've drawn up a contract for you. A real chunk of change. You'll see all the big cities of the world: Paris, London, New York... Just sign here, at the bottom of the page.

That's really nice, monsieur, but I'd rather stay with Monsieur Bodoni.

Ahaaa! I get it. You're a clever boy. You've got a nose for business. That's fine, I'll add 5% on the earnings. How about that?

No. It's not about money. I just want to help Monsieur Bodoni.

WHAT? You dare refuse such a contract! That's crazy! Nobody ever refuses a Choesels contract! NOW, SIGN HERE!
WAP

Come on, Mr. Choesels, don't insist. You see he's not interested and that--

WHAT ARE YOU POKING YOUR NOSE INTO? DO YOU HAVE A CONTRACT? NO! SO GET THE HECK AWAY FROM ME OR--

WUMP

I'm not forgetting about this, Bodoni! I want that show number and will get it! BY ANY MEANS NECESSARY!

?
VROAAR

What happened? Who's the screwball heading off bellowing like a bull?
That's Choesels!

He wanted to hire Benny, but he turned him down, so Choesels reacted badly, and Benny tossed him out!

You have to admit he had it coming to him! Didn't he, Monsieur Bodoni?
Agreed. But now we'll have to be on our guard.

Why? What are you afraid of?
You don't know Choesels. He'll do anything to get your act. Word to the wise: beware.

And the circus continues its triumphant tour...

Did you check the equipment?
Yes, it's fine. Everything's normal.

And what proves that these carrots for my bear aren't poisoned? Eh? You eat one!

BRAVO!
CLAP
CLAP
CLAP
Good! Nobody in the audience is trying to sabotage the show.
CLAP
CLAP
CLAP

We're sorry, Officer. We didn't know you were doing your rounds. We thought you were a prowler.
21

The days pass. Thanks to the box office receipts, performances are now happening under a larger big top, lit by a powerful generator. The animal collection grows in size, and new personnel is hired.

MOM, THEY'RE HERE TO DELIVER THE TV!

Hey, the circus is getting awesome, isn't it? You see? You were wrong to worry about Choesel's threats.
That's true.
Hey! Mister Bodoni!
US

John Nelaire, from the "Morning Gaul" newspaper, one million copies! I'd like to do a feature on your big star there, young Benny! I won't take long! All right? Okay! While we wait for my photographer, I'll go ahead and ask you a few questions!

Excuse me, but that's not possible at the moment. The show's starting soon. Can you come back afterwards?
That's difficult. No, it won't work! ...Unless he can come meet me this evening at the Commerce Hotel.

It's just--
Perfect, see you tonight! You'll see, it'll be sensational publicity!

That evening, after the show...
Yes, I know this feature is a good thing for the circus, but I don't want you going out by yourself at night. Pietro will go with you.

Don't be out too late!
I promise, Monsieur Bodoni!

Okay! One last question...
HOTEL DU COMMERCE

I saw your act! Impressive! But just between us, admit there's some trick!
No! Well, yes, I... uh...

A trick? Oh! Maybe there is, maybe not. And if there is one, you do understand he can't reveal it.

All right! Okay! Well, I have my feature! Did you finish with your photos?
Well, I'd have liked to have gotten one where you see him lifting something really heavy.

That's right! Let's see! What could we find?

What if we went back to the circus? There's a huge anvil there.
Hmm... no. We'd need something more original!

That's it! I got it! Come with me, guys!

My car is in the little street over there!

There it is!
052AD

Okay! Here's what I propose: Benny can slip under the car's front end and lift it! What do you all think of that? That'd be a great pic, wouldn't it? Agreed? Let's go, guys!

Good! Very good! Pietro, stand there on the side! Don't move! There! Now lift the car!
O52AD

Perfect! Turn this way! Good! One more!

Now, walk forward! No, don't smile! That's it! That's good!

Get me a close-up, George. One more.

Keep going, Benny! Yes! More!

Stop! That'll do, guys! You can set the car down, Benny!

It'll be an awesome print run! Okay, we'll say goodbye. We got to get back to the newspaper office tonight! I'll send you a few copies! Goodbye!

Whew! What a chatterbox.
Yes! Let's hurry back. It's getting late.

The next day, at dawn...
BOOM
BOOM
BOOM
BOOM
BOOM

Huh? What's this about?
Police! Sorry for dragging you out of bed, but I've been ordered to conduct a search of the premises. Here's the warrant.

What? I don't understand. There must be a mistake.
We'll see about that. Let's go!

What are you looking for? I don't have anything to hide. This whole thing is unbelievable.
Indeed!... Speaking of which, where were you last night between ten o'clock and midnight?

I was here!
Can you prove that?

Of course! Except for Benny and Pietro, who'd gone out, all the employees can vouch for me.
Ah-hah!

And I don't-- No! LOOK OUT! Don't touch that pian
BANG
KLINKLONK

All right! Call Benny and Pietro for me!

So, you say you spent the evening with two newspaper reporters from the "Morning Gaul." Okay, I'll check that out right away.

Do you hand out lots of free tickets?
No... just to the press and local authorities. Why?

No reason.

Ah! Here's my assistant returning with the newspaper's response.

The editor-in-chief was definite, Captain. He didn't send anyone to do a report on the circus.
Ah-hah!

But I swear it's true, Captain, sir!
The photographer's name was George!

We searched everywhere, Captain, but didn't find anything.
Too bad! Let's go!

Give me your tour itinerary so I'll know where to find you.

Do you understand anything about this?
No. It must be a mistake.
No doubt. Okay, back to work, guys.

Weird! Not the slightest trace of drugs and yet...
You were mistaken, Captain.

No, my friend. One of their own people exposed them. Look, he dropped a whole book of tickets in the car they used to do the job.

Goodness me! Why didn't you arrest them, in that case?
It's not enough proof. But patience, they'll end up making another little mistake. And then!...

Later...
BODONI
CIRCUS
TAXI

BODONI
It's here!
How much do I owe you?

There. Keep the change.
Thank you very much, sir!
What's a little money?
TAXI

The boss? He's near the red trailer. The one with a TV antenna.

Mister Bodoni?
Yes?

I'd like to show you a few photos taken yesterday by the reporters from the "Morning Gaul."
Good Heavens! I'm very happy to see you! You've brought proof Benny and Pietro were telling the police chief the truth!

It just so happens we had trouble with the police. I'll explain. Come, let's go see about this in my trailer.

Hey, there! Pietro, Benny! Come see the pics from the news-paper feature!

Would you like a drink?
Gladly!
27

Ah! They're good! I'd like to have some if possible.
They're all for you.

That's kind. Will you tell me how much I owe you?

A hundred thousand dollars!

A hundred thousand! HA! HA! Good one! You like jokes?
But that's not a joke, Mister Bodoni.

I see you haven't read the newspaper yet. Listen instead.

??
"A drug mystery. This morning, around five a.m., police found in a ditch near Lamotte-Saint-Guidon an American car with a 052AD license plate...

"In the car, which was stolen the night before from its owner, Mr. Kheu, Esq., several packets containing drugs were found. Alerted, drug enforcement agents have a lead and, according to Captain Arieu, who is leading the investigation, the traffickers will soon be arrested."

I don't understand. What's the connection between this matter and the photos?

Look in the newspaper at the car's license plate number.

A DRUG MYSTERY
You'll see it's the same as the one in your photos.

In these circumstances, you'll understand a hundred thousand dollars is barely anything. Unless you'd rather the police got ahold of these photos.
28

YOU CROOK! FRAUD! LOWLIFE!
POW

AAAH! TRYING TO BLACKMAIL ME? I'LL RETURN YOU TO SENDER INSTEAD!
Calm down, Dad!

You have three days to get the money! Or else you know what awaits you...

It's not true. We didn't steal a car, Monsieur Bodoni, I swear.
I know that, Benny. They lured you into a nice little trap. Ahh! They're clever.
We got to tell the police.

It's no use, they won't believe us. They'll figure we're trying to lead them astray to redirect the suspicion weighing on us.

But what'll we do then?
Pay up! We'll have to sell every-thing.
You'll be ruined.

I wonder if Choesels isn't behind all this!
You think so?

I'm going to find out! Pietro, tell your mother we're going!

BODONI
VROM
He'll pay dearly for it, if it's him!
29

CHOESELS
THE BIG CIRCUS IN THE
Okay, that'll work. Sign here. You'll start tomorrow.
Thank you, Mister Choesels, thanks again!

AND I'M TELLING YOU HE'LL SEE ME AND RIGHT NOW, TOO!
?

This is intolerable! I can't get any work done like this!

AAH! There you are, you crook! Admit you're the one who played that dirty trick on me!

Oh! Don't look all innocent. I know you were capable of something of the sort! But I promise you, you won't get away with it!
But, Bodoni, I don't understand! Explain yourself!
Uh... I see you're busy! I'll say goodbye!

Yikes! Things are getting heated in the boss's office!

...and don't come telling me you didn't organize that horrible blackmail!

That's not true, Bodoni. To prove it to you, I'll loan you the sum you need. How much did you say already?
30

All right, Bodoni, here's your check.
Oh! Mister Choesels... I'm embarrassed... and I thought you were the one who--

To do things by the book, I'll ask you to sign this IOU!
Of course!

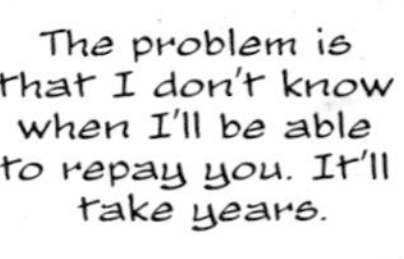
The problem is that I don't know when I'll be able to repay you. It'll take years.

Hmm... I know one way, but you might think I'm taking advantage of the situation.
No! No! Go ahead and say it. I'd do anything to prove my gratitude to you.

Well, what with the enormous resources at my disposal: Shows around the world, advertisements on all radio and TV channels, my international renown, and so on...

...it'd be enough for Benny to agree to work for me for one season, and I could consider your debt to me repaid. Of course, I'm just saying.

That'd be a solution obviously. But it's up to Benny. What do you think, Benny?
Well...

I don't know! I don't want to leave you, Monsieur Bodoni, but I'll say yes to Monsieur Choesels. It's the only way to sort things out!

AH! EXCELLENT! Go get your stuff fast and be here tomorrow morning. I'll see to everything else!

Hello! Get me New York!
Put together a press party for tomorrow!
Young woman, call in the radio and television folks.
And you call the photographer and printer.
Hello!
31

The next day...

CIRCUS CHOESELS

COMING SOON:
BENNY BREAKIRON
THE STRONGEST LITTLE BOY IN THE WORLD

Ladies and gentlemen, I introduce to you Benny Breakiron, the strongest little boy in the world!
Is he your phenom?
Over here! Thanks!
Oh! He's so cute! Woohoo!
There's some trick!
Of course!
CLIC

Is it true you're super strong?
People say there's a trick!
What do you think of fashion?
What trick?
CLIC

Would you like to go to the moon?
Do you know Brigitte Bardot?
So about that trick, huh?
Do you have a hobby?

The son of a Turkish father and a frail mother, he's the oldest of ten children. I found him among the dockworkers at the port of Anvers...

...where he was working very hard to... ... ...
...and then, my sister-in-law who, by the way, is not a wallflower, answered him right back...
Do you like Brahms?

That evening...
One last question, young Benny. Just between you and me, your strength isn't real? There's a trick? Can you tell us what?
Well, uh...

You don't want to say? Well, too bad! Thanks for being nice and coming to answer our questions. Good night!
Come on, Mona, it's time!

There aren't many people tonight. You can tell Benny is gone.
Yes, we'll have to revive our old numbers.

Wait! Aren't you afraid that once they have proof of the blackmail, Benny will return to work at Bodoni's?

There has to be a trick!

This kid's show number is awesome! It'll be a hit! The seats are already all sold out!

Bravo, Benny! Go get some rest now. You have to be tiptop for tonight's gala event!
Oui, Monsieur Choesels!

Here are the film and prints.
Here! That's a check and now get lost, you despicable man!
BODONI
BODONI

Bye now!

Heh heh heh! That imbecile Choesels made the check out to the bearer!
THE LAND OF THE SMURFS
TAXI

BANK
5%

Twenty-five and twenty-five: fifty! And fifty! One hundred! And...
TELL
5%

CIRCUS CHOESELS
BENNY BREAKIRON
THE STR
LITT
BENNY
BREAK

What's he up to? He's still not back with my check!
MISTER CHOESELS! I have a sick lion! What do we do?
BOSS! They want you at the refreshment stand!
MISTER CHOESELS! ...

Are you ready, Benny? Don't be nervous! The show manager will come call for you once it's time to go into the ring! All good?
Oui, Monsieur Choesels!

If I could only catch a cold!
HUM

Quick, boss, you're up! It's time!

GOOD EVENING, LADIES AND GENTLEMEN! Our big show tonight will start with...

The show is starting! Choesels must be center stage. I can go in without any risk.

CHOESELS CIRCUS

4

Ah! Here it is!
BENNY
36

NOK
NOK
NOK
Come in!

Good evening.
What are you doing here?

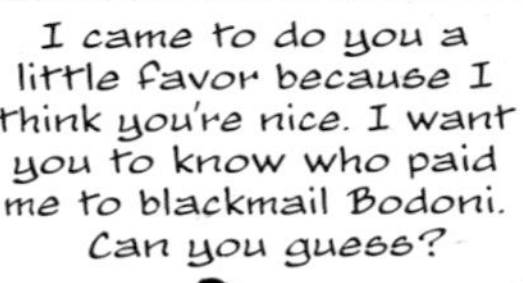
I came to do you a little favor because I think you're nice. I want you to know who paid me to blackmail Bodoni. Can you guess?

It was Choesels!
That's impossible! He's the one who gave Monsieur Bodoni the money to pay you.

Follow me and I'll show you the proof!
If you've lied to me, you'll regret it, cause I'm very strong!

Don't go far, Benny! You're up in five minutes!
No, I won't. I'll be right back.

Well? Where's the proof?
Shhh! Here in Choesel's office.
NOK
NOK

Nobody's here. Come in.

All right. Inside there's a set of the prints I was supposed to hand over to Bodoni.
Okay, we'll see about that. Let's go find Monsieur Choesels so he'll open his safe.
FORT

Certainly not! He'll find an excuse not to come and, at the first chance, he'll get rid of the proof of his guilt.

Fine, in that case, there's only one solution!

CROANG
37

CLAP
CLAP
BRAVO!
CLAP
CLAP
CLAP
CLAP

AND NOW, LADIES AND GENTLEMEN, HERE'S THE MOST EXTRAORDINARY, FANTASTIC SHOW YOU'VE EVER SEEN! THE STRONGEST LITTLE BOY IN THE WORLD! HERE'S...

BENNY!
TADAAAAAAA

BENNY!
TADAAAAAAA

Well?
Disappeared... he's not in his dressing room. I don't understand.

My dear audience, we're sorry, but our big star was feeling a little dizzy and we... uh... I... the veterinarian, uh... the doctor...
BOOOOOO
BOO!
BOO!

All right! There he is!
BOO!
BOOOOOO!
GIVE US OUR MONEY BACK!
BOOO!

IT'S GOOD NEWS: BENNY!
TADAAAAA

BANDIT!
?
38

I know everything! You're nothing but a crook! You were the one scheming with that dirty blackmailer!
But... but I don't understand!...

Oh, no? And these photos, then? What were they doing in your safe, huh? What's more, the blackmailer told me everything!
Come on, settle down! There are people here!

Well, even better! That way everyone will know you're a bad man! Because he's the one, ladies and gentlemen, who blackmailed Monsieur Bodoni with a photograph that wasn't from a real reporter and who put drugs in the car I didn't steal!

That's their fantastic show?
It's not even funny!
Yeah, it's weird!

Oh! Don't you think you're going to run away! You need to explain yourself to Monsieur Bodoni!

Next number, old friend! Next number!
And I'll tell the police, and you'll go to prison!

Lion tamer, in the ring! Quick, hurry it up, dang it!

Ready? Go ahead! Let the beasts in!

THE CAGING! We forgot the caging!
AAA!
BOOM
BANG
EEEEEEEEEEE
HELP! AAAAH!
EEEEEEEE

Luckily the blackmailer told me everything. He, at least, is honest!
I'm going to smash that chattering crow's face!

MY SAFE!
Hey, he's gone!

Bodoni's IOU! He took it!
?

MY CHECK!

Hello! Choesels here! Give me Mister Durant. Oh! That's you?... Yes, I know the bank's closed, but I got to put a stop payment on a check for a hundred thousand dollars that--

WHAT? CASHED!

But I don't understand! What's going on?
Oh, you've caused a fine mess! We're really up the creek!

But I know where he lives! He's going to return my money and quick, too!
CIRCUS

And I'm going to get back the IOU!
JEANS BOYS
TRUC

37!
That's it!
EEEEE

!
It's here?
EEEEEEEEEEEEEE

What are you doing here?
Uh, the same as you.

But I came to get back my money!
And me, the IOU!

GRMMBLBL!
37
DRIiiNG

Hello, miss, is Angelo Wiley in?
Oh, no! Mister Wiley just left!

Oh, yeah? Let's see for ourselves!
But I'm telling you...

Empty! He's flown the coop!
But I told you he'd left, sir.

He surely didn't tell you where he was going!
Yes, he did. I promised not to tell.
41

All right. How much?
How much what, sir? I don't understand.

Well, how much for giving me his address?
Oh! Sir! I want no part of that! I cannot be bought!

Yes, you can! How about that?
Oh! Oh!... Well.. Uh... in that case... uh well, here it is...!

Shhh, the kid musn't know. Whisper it in my ear!

Psss
Psss
Psss...

Speak up.
HE'S HARD OF HEARING!

Oh, really!...
I'M TO FORWARD HIS MAIL TO P.O. BOX 28 IN SAINT-ÉLEUTHÈRE!

You little brat! You'll pay for that!
Bonsoir, Mademoiselle! Good evening, Monsieur Choesels!

To the circus, fast! There's no time to lose. I'll pack my bags and hurry down there!
VROOM

Quick to Monsieur Bodoni's! I have to get there before Choesels!
42.

*The patron saint of lost things.

They're already here!

Look, Monsieur Bodoni, in front of the hotel, Choesels' car!
He's at the window! He saw us!
HOTEL
HOTEL DE LA

YOOHOO, Mister Choesels!
We're here!

VLAM

All right! While you keep an eye on the post office, Mona and I will go ask random people if they've seen him.
Be careful.

Let's go. Where do we start?
It doesn't matter! That hotel?

Look out! The kids are leaving! Tail them, Joe!

And don't you all just stand there! Find me that blackmailer! You have his sketch, don't you?

Okay, fellows, this won't be easy!
Hey! Look! There!
BEER

If he comes to get his mail here, I'll spot him!

THAT'S IT, BOSS! WE GOT HIM!
Already!?
44.

Here he is!
LET ME GO, YOU GANGSTERS! WHAT'S THE MATTER WITH YOU? I'M GOING TO MAKE A COMPLAINT!
!
?

YOU PACK OF FOOLS! LOOK AT MY DRAWING! YOU CAN SEE THAT'S NOT HIM!

He's a gentleman about fifty years old, dressed completely in black, with a black hat, and a little black beard.
And his name is Angelo Wiley, you say? No, he hasn't been here, young man.
CHÈQUE
HOTEL

Look, there's a restaurant at the end of the street. Maybe they've seen him there. Let's go ask.
HOTEL DU SUD
HÔTEL
PENSION

POSTE

LISEZ Spirou
"SYSTÈME"
Ask for our catalog
MORNING
NEW TRIBUNE
Style
5

It's getting late. Let's go back to Dad. Maybe he's had more luck than us.

Hey, have you noticed that man behind us? He's been following us for a good while.
45

?
He must be one of Choesels's goons! Listen, here's what we're going to do: PSSS psss...

Un, deux, trois... GO!

What... what's gotten into them?

That man runs well! It'll make him lose weight.
Come this way, Benny!

!
YIPPeee!

BAM

Where are they? Where are they?
DING DING DING

!
LISEZ SPIROU
7
SMOG FEET

HEY! STOP! -HUFF!-... WAIT FOR ME! -HUFF!-... TAXI!
46

LISEZ : SPIROU
7
SMOG FEET
TAVERNE
-PFF,- -PFF,- -PFF!- A stop... -PFF!- ...I ...I ...I'll catch it!...

Got it! -Whewww...-

Well, where are they?
Come on, Mona!
DING DING
LISEZ : SPIROU
SMOG FEET

OH, NOOOO!

Go that way!
I want off! Let me off! STOP FOR HEAVEN'S SAKE!

Don't do that, it's dangerous! You're going to BREAK YOUR--

BAM

...shtupid kidz... where did zhey go?

Look out, here he comes!
...

YOOHOO!

GL
GL
GL
GL
GALERIES LAFAILLITE
Is he still following us?
Yes, let's go inside!

Dang it, I can't lose them in this crowd!

Pardon me, sir!
Excuse me!
Pardon me, ma'am!
RÉCLAME

Come on! There's nobody after this lady!

Oh! Those rascals! They went up the escalator that's coming down!

Look out! Let me by!

HEY!
You're crazy!
You moron!
No pushing in back!
Keep moving up front!

AÏEOUCH!
Good heavens! My cake!
HELP!
MOMMY!
Oh! Sorry, mother dear!

Quick, the elevator! I absolutely must find them again!

There they are!
Ah! He finally found us again!
GLACES

DADDY'S PAYING!

GOÛTEZ NOS PARFAITS CRÈME CHANTILLY

I've lost sight of them once again!
100 SUPER BALLES

POW
100 SUPER BALLES

TCHAK
TOM
TOM
TCHING
BLING
TOM
GLING
TOM

A hundred! A hundred, sir!
A hundred? Are you kidding me? There's at least two million in damages!
HELP!
Seven years per mirror! I've rung up... uh, three hundred thirty-six years of bad luck!
CRAINGBLING
BLING
TCHING
BLING
TOM
TOM
49

MON
You go left, and I'll go right! We'll circle the block and meet on the far side!
Okay!

CAFÉ
?!

AVIS
Did he follow you?
No! It wasn't you?

That's not fair! We were having so much fun. Where did he go?
Look! There! On the bench!

BOO-HOOOO, I'VE HAD IT. ENOUGH! BOOO-HOOOO!

Come on, you shouldn't let yourself get upset like that.
Sniff!
We were just playing.

Come on, we're going to take you back.
And we'll be nice now.
...And he threatened to tell my wife everything! Which meant not only did I have to give him fifty bucks, he didn't pay his fare!
SUNC

Well, old friend, you ran into a blackmailer.
50

A blackmailer? His name's not Angelo Wiley, is it?
An ugly man dressed completely in black.

That's him! With a little goatee, right? You know him?
Oui, you don't know where he lives, do you?

I dropped him off at 6A Rue de Fêves. That's close by. The third street on the left. After the roundabout over there.

Merci, monsieur!
6A Rue de Fêves!

6A Rue de Fêves!

Quick, the phone!
In the back.

Choesels will be happy, but he'll have to hurry to get there before the kids do!
ODM
DÉMOB.
353532
187742

Busy!
TUUUT
TUUUT
TUUUT

RUE DES FÊVES
It's here!

Ah! It's ringing!... Hello? Postal Hotel?... Connect me to Mister Choesels's room!... Hello? Oh! It's you, Emile? Put Choesels on!

He's taking his bath!... What?... Wait, I'll jot this down!
51

MISTER CHOESELS, Joe just called! He says he knows where the blackmailer lives!
Leave the address for me and hurry over there in my car! I'll take a taxi to meet you!

Do you know where Rue de Fêves is?
Nope!
We'll ask!
VAROOM
LA POSTE

Mister Angelo Wiley? Fifth floor, first door on the left!

This is it!
NOK
NOK
NOK

What...?

SLAM
CRIC
CRAC

CRAAC

6A Rue de Fêves? Let's see!... You could go via the train station, but that'd be out of your way. No! Take the third... uh... no, the fourth right. Or instead... wait, I think there's a simpler way...

Mister Benny! What a nice surprise. But do come on in. To what do I owe the pleasure of your visit?

The IOU! And the money! Quick!

The IOU? But I don't know what you're talking about, Mister Benny. You ought to talk with Mister Choesels instead.

WHAT? LOOK OUT, CAUSE I'M GOING TO GET MAD!

TAXI! HEY, TAXI!
POSTE
BAZAR DU COIN

6A Rue de Fèves!
Z

So you still don't want to tell where you hid the IOU?

You're really don't want to, huh?

Sure about that?...

Yes, yes, I'll give it to you.

Hurry up, blast it!
Yeah, yeah, whatever!

It's here in this cabinet.
My soapy water!

I don't see it. Oh! Yes, here it is!

SPLASH

Oww! My eyes! That stings!

Where is he?
He ran away, but don't worry. We'll catch him again soon. Wipe off!

Wait, you're soaking wet!
No! Come on!

We're too late! He's almost at the bottom!

Well, I'll get there before he does! I know a shortcut.

Fourth... third... second...

Ground floor!
TCHOC
54

Split it?

Oh, alright!

It's here!
There's Joe!

You sure took your time! The housekeeper told me the kids were up there!
Fine, let's go!

Are you Angelo Wiley?
Yes, how may I help you?

THE MONEY! AND THE IOU!
Uh... Mister Benny is the one who has them.

Give me that briefcase, kid!
No!

WHAT? Give me that right now, or I'll give you a smack!

Oh, don't you try it! I'm very strong and won't let you push me around!
55

POW
I warned you!

Sic them! Go on!
Surround him! I'll grab the briefcase!

POW
POW

Keep the change!
TAXI

Do you want to take it from me, too?
No, no, Mister Benny!

That's good. Scram, but if I ever-- a... a...
...A

ATCHOOO!

Oh, Zut! A cold! It's because of that soapy water! And now I've lost all my strength!

Angelo Wiley is on which floor?
Five!
Choesels!
56

?
I have to find another way out!

!?

WHAT HAP-PENED?
It was young Benny! He went back upstairs with the money in a briefcase!

!

Quick, Mona, let's run! Choesels is here!
Why run, Benny? You're stronger than he is!

No, I just caught a cold and when I have one, I lose all my strength!

Yikes! We're in the attic!
Uh, oh! He's coming!

Here! This one is open!

Quick! Get the lock!
CLAC

What now?
Well, uh..
OPEN UP!
BAMM
BAMM

OPEN IT! OR I'LL BUST THE DOOR DOWN!

Come on, I've found the way to get away from him!
?

Look! That's how we'll get away! Give me your hand!
!

Don't be afraid! Whatever you do, don't look down!

Be brave. You're almost there!

You okay?
I'm... I'm okay!...

Ah! You refuse to open it? That's fine!
I'M BUSTING THE DOOR IN!

Are they there? Do you want a hand?

We're lucky, there's an open skylight!
58

Oh? Okay!...
KRAAK

Whew!

They escaped through the rooftops!

Where did they go?

Hey there, Dad! We did it! We got the IOU!
!

Good job, kids! But how did you do that? Tell me!
ATCHOOOOO!
Bless you, Benny!
VROOM

Later...
Let myself get outwitted by kids! Me, Choesels!
$100,000 blown! I'll go bankrupt!

Mister Choesels! Mister Bodoni is here!
What? What does he want from me?

What do you want? Fine! I lost! That's no reason to come here and rub it in my face! If an apology is what you want, fine, you have it! There! Are you happy?

Choesels, you didn't do us right maybe, but this money belongs to you!
We came to give it back to you!

And a few days later...

Peyo, Walthéry & Gos

WATCH OUT FOR PAPERCUTZ

Welcome to the second smurftastic volume of THE SMURFS TALES by Peyo—the new Smurfs graphic novel series that picks up where THE SMURFS left off. In other words, Papercutz, the very same folks dedicated to publishing great graphic novels for all ages, had been publishing THE SMURFS for 26 volumes, not counting special editions or such series as THE SMURFS ANTHOLOGY or THE SMURFS 3 IN 1, and decided to relaunch the series as THE SMURFS TALES for the following fun reasons...

To tie-in to the all-new Smurfs animated series on Nickelodeon. This new cartoon series will undoubtedly create greater awareness of the Smurfs in general, and we wanted new Smurfs fans to be able to get in on the fun with a new graphic novel series, rather than start with volume 27 of the previous series.

The trend in graphic novels has been to offer more and more pages in each graphic novel, so how could we resist the opportunity to not only offer more Smurfs in every graphic novel, but to also feature other great Peyo characters such as *Johan and Peewit* and *Benny Breakiron*?

So, that's the story behind THE SMURFS TALES. But for those of you wondering who *Peyo, Benny Breakiron, and Johan and Peewit* are, allow me, Jim Salicrup, the Smurf-in-Chief to answer those questions...

Peyo is the name cartoonist Pierre Culliford used when creating his comics. While many people believe the Smurfs started as animated cartoons back in the 80s, the truth is that they started as comics in 1958, when they popped up as characters in the *Johan and Peewit* comic by Peyo.

Benny Breakiron is yet another comic created by Peyo. Perhaps inspired by Superman, *Benny* is a young French boy with super powers. But if *Benny* should catch a cold, his super powers go away until he gets over his cold. *Benny* previously had his own Papercutz series for four volumes, and returns here in THE SMURFS TALES.

Johan and Peewit are a couple of medieval characters—a royal page and a court jester, respectively—who star in their own comedy/adventure series created by Peyo. It was in their 1958 adventure, "The Flute with Six Holes," that they met the Smurfs. In THE SMURFS TALES Volume One, they were featured in two stories, and they'll be returning soon.

That should answer most of your questions about the Smurfs. If you want to enjoy earlier Smurfs comics look for THE SMURFS 3 IN 1 which is re-presenting the earlier SMURFS graphic novels, three at a time. For earlier adventures of *Benny Breakiron* look for THE SMURFS AND FRIENDS graphic novels. For earlier *Johan and Peewit* stories look for THE SMURFS AND FRIENDS and THE SMURFS ANTHOLOGY. You may find these at booksellers and libraries everywhere. Just don't forget about THE SMURFS TALES Volume Three is coming soon and we don't want you to miss it!

Smurf you later,

Jim

STAY IN TOUCH!

EMAIL:	salicrup@papercutz.com
WEB:	papercutz.com
TWITTER:	@papercutzgn
INSTAGRAM:	@papercutzgn
FACEBOOK:	PAPERCUTZGRAPHICNOVELS
FANMAIL:	Papercutz, 160 Broadway, Suite 700, East Wing, New York, NY 10038

Go to papercutz.com and sign up for the free Papercutz e-newsletter!

SMURFS GRAPHIC NOVELS AVAILABLE FROM PAPERCUTZ™

1. THE PURPLE SMURFS

2. THE SMURFS AND THE MAGIC FLUTE

3. THE SMURF KING

4. THE SMURFETTE

5. THE SMURFS AND THE EGG

6. THE SMURFS AND THE HOWLIBIRD

7. THE ASTROSMURF

8. THE SMURF APPRENTICE

9. GARGAMEL AND THE SMURFS

10. THE RETURN OF THE SMURFETTE

11. THE SMURF OLYMPICS

12. SMURF VS. SMURF

13. SMURF SOUP

14. THE BABY SMURF

15. THE SMURFLINGS

16. THE AEROSMURF

17. THE STRANGE AWAKENING OF LAZY SMURF

18. THE FINANCE SMURF

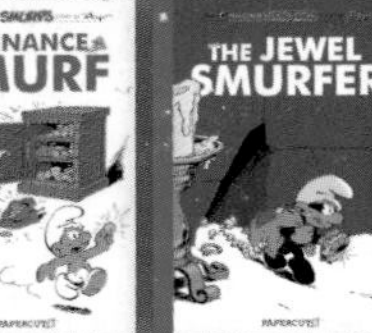

19. THE JEWEL SMURFER

20. DOCTOR SMURF

21. THE WILD SMURF

22. THE SMURF MENACE

23. CAN'T SMURF PROGRESS

24. THE SMURF REPORTER

25. THE GAMBLING SMURFS

26. SMURF SALAD

THE SMURFS 3 IN 1 VOL. 1

THE SMURFS 3 IN 1 VOL. 2

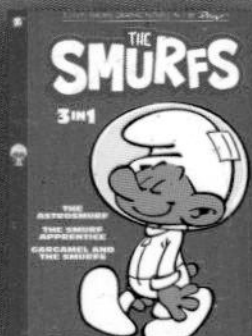

THE SMURFS 3 IN 1 VOL. 3

THE SMURFS 3 IN 1 VOL. 4

-THE VILLAGE BEHIND THE WALL

THE BETRAYAL OF SMURF-BLOSSOM

THE SMURFS CHRISTMAS

FOREVER SMURFETTE

SMURFS MONSTERS

THE SMURFS TALES VOL.1

THE SMURFS TALES VOL.2

THE SMURFS graphic novels are available in paperback for $5.99 each and in hardcover for $10.99 each, except for THE SMURFS #21-#26, and THE VILLAGE BEHIND THE WALL, which are $7.99 each in paperback and $12.99 each in hardcover, at booksellers everywhere. THE SMURFS 3 IN 1 are in paperback only for $14.99 each. THE VILLAGE BEHIND THE WALL 2: THE BETRAYAL OF SMURFBLOSSOM is $12.99 each in hardcover only. THE SMURFS TALES are available in paperback for $14.99 each and in hardcover for $22.99 each. You can also order online at papercutz.com. Or call 1-800-886-1223, Monday through Friday, 9 – 5 EST. MC, Visa, and AmEx accepted. To order by mail, please add $5.00 for postage and handling for first book ordered, $1.00 for each additional book and make check payable to NBM Publishing. Send to: Papercutz, 160 Broadway, Suite 700, East Wing, New York, NY 10038.

THE SMURFS graphic novels are also available digitally wherever e-books are sold.

PAPERCUTZ.COM